Secret Notebook of SHERLOCK HOLMES

Liz Hedgecock

WHITE
RHINO
BOOKS

ISBN: 1532813686
ISBN-13: 978-1532813689

For Stephen, who made it possible.

Contents

Foreword

Professor J. Parker Holcroft
Department of Criminology
University of Westmorland

The Secret Notebook of Sherlock Holmes is an important addition to our canon of Sherlock Holmes case literature. At first I was certain that the newly-discovered notebook, in which Dr Watson records several hitherto-unknown early cases, was a fake. However, having read the volume from cover to cover, and subjected it to a battery of tests, I am confident that the *Notebook* is indeed the genuine article.

The circumstances of the *Notebook*'s discovery are well-known. Students of criminology will have viewed the BBC News coverage and the *Antiques Roadshow* special, in addition to reading my definitive monograph on the subject. For the less well-informed reader, the

1

Notebook was found on Tuesday 16th February 2016 at 221B Baker Street, the former residence of Sherlock Holmes. The rooms are preserved as a museum to the master detective, and as far as possible Holmes's relics have been retained there.

Sherlock Holmes himself would have noted some peculiarities about Tuesday 16th February. It was a particularly wet and miserable day, falling within the English schools' half-term holiday. These factors led to high visitor numbers at 221B Baker Street, with a greater than usual number of bored school-age children. One of these, a Miss Jessica Farley, took it upon herself first to open and then to rummage in Sherlock Holmes's sock drawer, while her parents examined a display of pipes and other smoking paraphernalia in the sitting room. By Miss Farley's own account, the *Notebook* was 'shoved right to the back, under the drawer lining'. Miss Farley's parents were drawn back to the room by their daughter's giggles as she perused the book. Fortunately for all concerned, and for the future of Sherlock Holmes scholarship, a museum attendant hurried to the book's rescue before it was torn in two by a most unseemly tug-of-war.

When I was informed of the find, I was convinced that the *Notebook* was a forgery planted by an audacious visitor. I ordered that the book should undergo testing, expecting it to be unmasked within days. This proved not to be the case.

The notebook appears genuine; a standard red leather notebook of a type available during the period when Dr Watson would have kept his journal, and carbon dating confirmed this. The ink used throughout the notebook is Stephens' indelible blue-black writing fluid. This matches with other notebooks in the possession of the Department of Criminology containing Watson's case notes and rough drafts. Finally, experts at the University of Westmorland conducted a graphological and linguistic analysis of the text. Dr Watson's handwriting is not as fully formed as in the later notebooks in our archives, but it is still recognisably his. The style also differs from the prose of Dr Watson's *Strand Magazine* articles. However, this is usual in a private notebook, and where all other indicators declare the *Notebook*'s authenticity, it would be churlish to refute it on the basis of some minor stylistic inconsistencies.

The differences between the *Notebook* and Watson's later writings may also explain why its existence has only just come to light. Watson is far less reverential towards his friend in the *Notebook* than in his other writings. Perhaps more importantly, Holmes does not solve all the cases in the *Notebook*. The insight this provides into the development of Holmes's skills is invaluable, for these early cases are Holmes's training-ground.

The majority of the cases recorded in the *Notebook* fall

into the period before Holmes's prime, which is considered to begin in 1886, and among these are several less prestigious cases which Holmes took on before his reputation was established. These suggest that late-Victorian London may have been less sinister and criminal than is commonly thought, since many of them arise from misinterpretation rather than evil intent.

The most convincing hypothesis proposed to date for the *Notebook*'s disappearance is that Holmes himself concealed it in his sock drawer. If this is correct, it suggests that Holmes had a hitherto unsuspected interest in safeguarding his public image. This raises another question; why did Holmes keep the *Notebook*, rather than destroying it? There are many possible answers: a sentimental attachment to Watson's writing; a desire to preserve the complete record of his case histories; or perhaps to retain the memory of his less successful days, as a check and balance to the image of 'the great detective'.

To conclude, *The Secret Notebook of Sherlock Holmes* raises many questions which we cannot yet answer. This edition has been rushed out to meet public demand, following the news of the discovery. However, I am at present preparing an annotated facsimile edition of the *Notebook* which will, I hope, lift the veil of mystery currently draped over this extraordinary book.

The Case of the Yellow Book

I watched as Sherlock Holmes, eyes narrowed, released a drop from his pipette into a flask of colourless liquid. There was a fizz, a puff of smoke, and the flask's contents turned electric blue.

'Amazing, Holmes!' I cried. 'What does it do?'

'Absolutely nothing,' Holmes smiled. 'But it is rather attractive, don't you think?'

I coughed as a pungent smell wafted towards me. 'The aroma, less so.' The front door bell jangled heartily and I flapped at the air in front of me. 'Sometimes, Holmes, your timing is as off as your experiments.'

Billy the page appeared moments later, smirking. 'Pleased to announce Mr . . . er . . . '

'Wilde. Oscar Wilde.' The owner of the name stepped forward with a flourish of his bowler hat. He was a tall, broad-shouldered young man, wearing rather

5

a loud checked suit. 'Do I have the honour of addressing Mr Sherlock Holmes?'

'You do indeed,' Holmes said, looking him up and down.

'I see that you are sizing me up,' the young man observed with a smile. 'Indeed, people who judge by appearances are the only sensible ones — no! That wasn't it!' He frowned. 'I may as well come to the point. My notebook, full of epigrams which I have polished to a high shine, has been stolen!'

'Your notebook?' I asked, mystified.

'Yes. I am a writer . . . a poet at present, and a student, but one day I hope to write plays, novels . . . ' He waved his hands in the air as if conducting an orchestra, then froze. 'But without my book, I am lost!'

'Hmm.' Holmes steepled his fingers and closed his eyes. 'When did you last see the book?'

'Two days ago. I took it out to make a note about a swallow and a jewel. I made a regrettable blot in the second line which I would give my eye-teeth to see again!' Wilde's expression of woe would have been almost comical if it had not been obvious how deeply he was affected.

'I hope that will not be necessary,' said Holmes. 'Where do you usually keep the book?'

'Next to my heart, in the inside pocket of my jacket.'

'Of course. And did you replace the book there when you made the note?'

Wilde's brow furrowed with the effort of recall. 'No — I left it on the table next to me, in my rooms at Magdalen. I sensed that inspiration would strike again, and I did not want to waste time. Oh!' He put his head in his hands. 'What a fool I was!'

'Mr Wilde, please try not to worry. I am sure that we can recover your book.' Holmes regarded the young man over his steepled fingers. 'What does it look like?'

'It is of an ordinary size, but its binding is a vivid dandelion yellow. Even the humblest flowers may have their own beauty.' Wilde's hand automatically went to his pocket, and he winced.

'And what have your activities been between the last time you saw the book and the moment when you missed it?'

'Let me see . . . I made the note and put the book down. Ah, and then my aunt arrived unexpectedly!' Wilde grinned. 'She likes to surprise me and take me out to tea. She worries that I don't get enough to eat at college.'

Holmes's face brightened. 'Indeed! And where did you go for your tea?'

'To a tearoom near the college with a wonderful Madeira cake. I have already enquired for my book there, to no avail.'

'And after that?'

'I walked Aunt Mabel to the station to catch the London train. We had to rush rather as she had a ticket for the opera.' Wilde smiled fondly. 'She's a wonderful woman, Aunt Mabel. Formidable. Seventy-two and sharp as a hatpin.'

'Does she encourage you in your literary career, Mr Wilde?'

'Not exactly.' Wilde crossed one leg over the other, revealing a sock patterned entirely at odds with his suit. 'Aunt Mabel only reads popular novels. I presented her with a volume of my poetry once, and she looked over her lorgnette at me — oh, with such an expression on her face!' Wilde chuckled.

'Mm.' Holmes pondered. 'I would like to have a conversation with your aunt, Mr Wilde.'

Wilde's mouth dropped open. 'You cannot believe that Aunt Mabel is the thief!'

'No, no, not at all. But a theory is forming in my mind. What happened after you saw your aunt off at the station?'

'I strolled by the river for perhaps half an hour, and then walked back to my rooms and read. I only missed the notebook yesterday morning, when I woke with a beautiful thought — alas, it is gone now. I have retraced my steps a hundred times, and asked at the porter's lodge and the station, but no book has been found.'

'There was no sign that anyone had forced their way into your room?'

Wilde laughed without merriment. 'Absolutely not.'

'Then I would definitely like to speak with your aunt.

Does she live in London?'

'No, in Brighton. I believe she is going back by the train today; she said she would stay with an old schoolfriend for a day or two, and the Sunday service is frightful.' Oscar Wilde's face brightened as he checked his watch. 'Indeed, you might catch her at the station. She usually catches the fast train at ten to four.'

Holmes leapt up. 'Let us go!' Wilde sprang after him, and I followed at a pace only marginally more sedate. I had no idea what Holmes's theory was, or how he had arrived at it, but I trusted him completely; and it appeared that Oscar Wilde did too.

We jumped into a cab and reached Victoria Station in less than fifteen minutes, shaken but undamaged. 'Half-past three! Where are we likely to find your aunt, Mr Wilde?'

'In the tea-room, consuming a cup of Earl Grey tea and a slice of Dundee cake,' Wilde replied immediately. 'The game is afoot, Mr Holmes!' He raced off with Holmes and me in his wake. 'There she is!' He indicated a well-dressed elderly lady with an enormous black handbag on the chair beside her. Protruding from the handbag was a yellow-jacketed book.

'Aunt Mabel! I — oh!' Wilde stopped dead as he spied the book.

'Oscar!' Aunt Mabel put her cup down. 'Is something wrong? You look haunted, dear boy!'

'I believe I can explain,' said Holmes, stepping

forward. 'Excuse me, dear lady, but your nephew Mr Wilde discovered that you had mistaken his book for your yellowback novel. He hurried here to return your book, but in his haste he has forgotten it. I will purchase another copy from the bookstall, for you to read on the train home.'

Aunt Mabel fixed Holmes with a steely stare. 'Well,' she said, 'that would be extremely kind of you, Mr . . . '

'Holmes. Mr Sherlock Holmes.' The great detective had blushed to the roots of his hair, and was shifting from foot to foot like a schoolboy in the headmaster's office.

'Indeed. I was reading *The Last of the Mortimers*, by Mrs Oliphant.'

'An excellent choice,' said Holmes, and ran away to the bookstall.

'May I have my book, Aunt Mabel?' asked Wilde, eyeing his notebook as a blackbird eyes her eggs when a fox is near.

'Of course, dear boy.' Aunt Mabel presented it back to him like a prize. 'I did think that the narrative had taken a most unexpected turn.'

'There are some rather fine passages,' said Wilde. He tucked the book into his pocket and patted it, then kissed his aunt's hand. 'Goodbye, Aunt Mabel.'

'Goodbye, dear boy.' Aunt Mabel took her novel from Holmes and swept off to the train platform, where the guard raised his hat to her.

'Well, Mr Wilde, that was elementary,' said Holmes.

'Really, Holmes?' I said.

Holmes laughed. 'Yes! The colour of the notebook was the first significant point. Mr Wilde, when you told me your aunt read novels, used a lorgnette, and travelled by train, everything fell into place. Clearly she had taken your yellow notebook instead of her own yellowback novel, bought at the station bookstall for the journey. I must say in earnest, though, that at the beginning of your case I had not deduced that the answer would lie in a handbag at Victoria Station.'

'A handbag?' said Oscar Wilde. 'A handbag!' He beamed, reached into his jacket pocket, and scribbled a new note in his yellow book.

The Case of the Royal Lineage

'Well, Mrs Hudson did us proud,' I remarked, brushing crumbs from my waistcoat. 'That was a breakfast of champions.'

'It was, rather.' Holmes put his knife and fork together. 'I feel a brisk walk is in order.'

There was a loud bang on the front door. 'I fancy we may need to postpone the walk,' said Holmes. 'That is the sort of knock which means business. Now, is there any egg yolk on my tie?'

Billy appeared at the dining-room door. 'Mr Lumsden,' he announced, and made himself scarce.

Mr Lumsden was a horsy-looking, weatherbeaten man of perhaps forty. 'Mr Holmes, I'm very glad you're in,' he said, striding across the room and gripping Holmes's hand. 'I do believe you're the only man who can help.'

'I will do my best,' said Holmes, smugly. 'What sort

of matter is it?'

'A most delicate one,' the man said, lowering his voice. 'The Queen's Pomeranian is in heat again!'

'What!' I exclaimed, and sidled towards the poker in case the man turned violent.

Mr Lumsden laughed and held up his hands. 'I must apologise,' he said. 'I should have introduced myself more fully. I am Queen Victoria's veterinary surgeon.'

'But what does this have to do with me?' Holmes enquired.

'Well, initially I approached Inspector Lestrade about the case, but he said that it would be a waste of police time . . . ' Mr Lumsden's voice faltered as he caught the full force of Holmes's thunderous glare. 'Look, Gena's had three litters of puppies now, and we don't know who the father is! It's completely messing up our breeding programme!'

'Ah!' Holmes settled back in his chair with an enigmatic smile. 'I presume the dog is under close watch?'

'Of course; she is occupied most of the day with walks and play-time.'

'And at night?'

'She is in the kennel with the other dogs.'

'Would I be right in thinking that you suspect some sort of night-time skulduggery?'

Mr Lumsden's face brightened. 'That's exactly it!'

Holmes inclined his head. 'Very well,' he intoned.

'We will convene at the kennels this evening and await developments.'

*

'Give me some of that brandy, Watson, I'm frozen to the bone.' I passed Holmes my flask, and we watched the morning mist rise over the estate.

'We were so sure,' muttered Holmes. 'But the dog did nothing in the night-time!' He took another pull at the flask. 'She was probably exhausted from biting me.' Holmes and Gena, it was fair to say, had not taken to each other.

'Perhaps we will pick up another lead,' I said. Holmes scowled.

We kept a close eye on the kennel, observing the kennel maids as they brought the dogs' breakfast. Still nothing untoward happened. Then whistling cut through the barking, and a young man in livery appeared. 'Walkies!' he cried. One of the kennel maids appeared, towed by three dogs including Gena, a yapping white fluff-ball who was trying to nip the others. The kennel maid handed Gena's lead to the footman.

'Here we go!' whispered Holmes.

'It won't be a long walk,' I said. 'That dog's hardly got any legs.'

We tailed the footman as he strolled towards the gate, still whistling. When he reached the gate he bent and retrieved a long coat and a basket from under the hedge. He donned the coat, bundled the dog into the basket, and turned left out of the gate. Holmes and I followed, keeping well back. Then the footman hailed an omnibus and climbed to the top deck.

'What shall we do?' I cried. 'He'll spot us if we board!'

'We'll hitch,' said Holmes. 'Not yet . . . Now!'

As the omnibus moved off we burst from the gate and sprinted. Holmes gained a narrow lead, grabbed the stair rail, and crouched low. I ran as fast as I could, but the omnibus was picking up speed. 'Go on without me, Holmes!' I panted.

'Never!' Holmes cried. He leaned back, and stretched out his hand. I grasped it thankfully, and Holmes heaved me onto the rail beside him.

Two minutes later the omnibus began to slow. 'Drop!' hissed Holmes, and we scurried behind a convenient large bush nearby. Our man got down and strolled off, and we resumed our erratic pursuit. After a couple of twists and turns, the footman walked down the garden path of a pleasant villa in open grounds. Yet instead of ringing the bell, he continued on round the side of the house. 'Uncle George!' we heard him call. 'I've got 'er!' A fusillade of barking greeted his shout.

'Come, Watson,' said Holmes, straightening his tie. 'We will finish this!' As we approached the front door I spied the small brass plate affixed to it. 'Mr Geo. Banting, Breeder. Kennel Club Affiliate.'

Holmes gasped. 'The effrontery!'

We tiptoed to the back of the house and peeped round the corner just as a tweed-suited man held up a squirming white Pomeranian. 'How about this one, Fred?' he said to the footman. 'They should make a nice litter. We'll get that Royal Warrant yet!' The footman nodded, and his hand moved to the fastening of his basket.

Holmes broke cover, bellowing 'This is an outrage!', and rugby-tackled the footman to the ground. The basket burst open and a yapping, furious Gena shot out, ran straight to Holmes, and bit him on the nose.

*

Holmes received a special medal for services to the crown, although it didn't stop him moaning. 'They're lucky it hasn't left a scar,' he grumbled, fingering his nose tenderly.

'Well, the dog had been through quite an ordeal,' I said. 'And at least the royal breeding programme is saved.'

'True, true . . . '

'Didn't Mr Lumsden offer you a pup from the litter, by the way?'

'He did,' growled Holmes. 'I turned it down.'

The Case of the Pea-Souper

Handkerchiefs to our noses, Holmes and I stumbled through the door of 221B Baker Street, drawing in deep lungfuls of the boiled-cabbage aroma issuing from the kitchen.

London was in the grip of a miserable fog, a real pea-souper. It had beset the city for days, smothering the streets in a foul-smelling blanket thick enough to cut with a knife. You could barely move for shouts and curses as people barged into each other, like an enormous game of blind-man's-buff.

Seconds after our arrival there was a thump on the door, followed by a muttered swearword and a loud knock. I opened the door and peered at the epaulettes and brass buttons glinting in the gloom.

'Is Mr Holmes there?' asked a husky voice.

'Scroggins!' boomed Holmes, extending a hand. 'How goes it?'

'Terrible, sir, terrible!' Scroggins replied. 'You're my last hope, sir!'

'Oh come now!' Holmes laughed. 'I provided Scroggins here with some small assistance in a case involving the Prussian Embassy's marmalade cat,' he explained. 'He is their doorman.'

'This is much worse!' exclaimed Scroggins. 'This time I've lost an ambassador!'

'That is rather careless,' said Holmes, filling his pipe. 'What are the circumstances?'

'Our new ambassador, Count Keller, asked me to recommend a restaurant for lunch. I suggested Simpson's-in-the-Strand.'

'Of course,' said Holmes.

'At three o'clock a messenger boy came from the restaurant, and said the Ambassador had lunched so well that he couldn't walk back, and they would put him into a hansom cab. But he never arrived!'

'Is the Count familiar with London?'

'It's his first visit, sir.' Scroggins wrung his hands.

Holmes glanced at his watch. 'Two hours have passed. We will accompany you, and see what we can discover.'

An hour later Holmes had questioned the whole staff, muddied his knees examining the cobbles outside the restaurant, and searched both locations from top to bottom. We stood on the embassy steps, thoroughly flummoxed. 'There's nothing for it,' he said, putting a filthy hand on Scroggins' shoulder. 'We must alert Scotland Yard.'

Scroggins gulped.

'Did you hear that?' I said.

'What?' asked Holmes, testily.

'That . . . clopping.'

The faint rhythm grew louder, and a dark shape advanced towards us in the swirling fog. Five feet away, the apparition became a horse pulling a hansom cab.

Scroggins leapt to the window. 'It's him!' he cried. We peered inside and our eyes met the flattened, open-mouthed face of Count Keller, sound asleep.

'What happened?' Holmes shouted up to the cabman. 'Did you meet with an accident?'

'No, sir!' the cabman shouted back cheerfully. 'We've been on a lovely trip!'

Holmes's eyes narrowed. 'Am I to understand that you've taken the gentleman on a tour?'

The cabman grinned. 'Well, as it was his first time in London I showed him the sights. Very scenic city,' he said, waving a hand at the dense grey mist.

Holmes sighed. 'Give the Ambassador a hand out, will you.'

'Righto!' The cabman jumped down. 'There's just the matter of my fare . . . two guineas should do it.'

Scroggins looked imploringly at Holmes, who sighed and fished in his pockets. 'Scroggins, the next time you lose someone — '

'Yes, sir?'

'Don't call on me.'

The Malady of
Sherlock Holmes

Sherlock Holmes got up from the breakfast table with a face like thunder, and rang the bell.

'Mrs Hudson,' he seethed, 'this egg is practically hard-boiled. Please remove it and bring an egg that I can insert a spoon into without snapping it.'

Mrs Hudson glared at Holmes, picked up the egg-cup, and left the room.

I bit the head off my toast soldier. 'Any good cases on the books?'

'Nothing,' spat Holmes. 'All the criminals appear to have gone to the seaside.' He retreated behind a copy of the *Times*, and I noticed that his hands were shaking violently.

'Are you all right, Holmes?'

Holmes lowered the paper and glared at me. 'Never

better.'

Mrs Hudson came in with a second egg. Holmes tested it with his spoon, snarled, and threw it against the wall.

*

I observed Holmes as closely as I dared for the rest of the day. This was easier than usual because he spent the day huddled in his armchair, shivering, sweating, and complaining of a headache.

'I wish you would let me examine you,' I said. 'I am a doctor, after all.'

'Go away,' said Holmes, burrowing further into the chair until it was difficult to ascertain where dressing-gown ended and upholstery began.

Mrs Hudson came in bearing a tray with a steaming cup of beef-tea and a bowl of tapioca pudding, as per my secret instructions. Holmes shuddered and turned away.

'It'll do you good, Mr Holmes,' she admonished.

'I doubt it,' Holmes said, darkly.

Mrs Hudson put the tray down. 'Can you try and make sure he eats some of it, Dr Watson? We can't have him wasting away.'

'I'll do my best, Mrs Hudson.' She nodded, flinging a half-contemptuous, half-triumphant glance at the oblivious Holmes.

Uneasiness crept into my mind. Holmes's illness, and Mrs Hudson's reaction, had started a disturbing train of thought. Holmes may be the detective, but my own grey matter is not inconsiderable. What if —

What if Mrs Hudson was poisoning Holmes?

I rebuked myself instantly, but the suspicion was in my head now. Holmes's symptoms — shaking, sweating, ill-temper — had appeared with a strange suddenness. Besides, Holmes's refusal of food was most uncharacteristic; in general, he ate like a horse. I recalled his reaction to the tray of food. Holmes knew all was not right; and he was shielding Mrs Hudson!

But what might our landlady's motive be for such a terrible deed? My eye caught the VR monogrammed on the wall in bullet holes, and I reflected on the violin-playing at all hours, the succession of strange callers, and the numerous police visits. Holmes was in no way a model tenant.

Now I just need to prove my case, I thought. I would taste the food on the tray, and catch the poisoner! I sipped the beef-tea, and took a spoonful of the pudding. Both tasted normal; rather good, in fact. Then I remembered Mrs Hudson's malevolent look at breakfast. Perhaps she knew I suspected her, and was planning to resume her evil regime later that day.

At supper time another tray duly appeared, this time with a broiled mutton chop, mashed potatoes, and peas. Holmes shook his head and clutched his stomach, and a tear rolled down his cheek. I watched in anguish, unable to bear the sight of such a noble man reduced to a quaking wreck.

'I can stand it no longer,' he whispered, and opened the drawer of the occasional table. The drawer where he kept his pistol.

'Holmes, no!'

I dived to stop him, but it was too late. Holmes's hand emerged clutching his briar pipe. He retrieved some tobacco from the Persian slipper, filled the pipe, and as a plume of acrid smoke polluted the air, Holmes was instantly restored to health.

The Biter Bit

'Late for a visit,' remarked Holmes, in response to the peal of the door-bell. 'This can be no mundane matter. Watson, will you do me the honour of remaining a little longer?' I had intended to get home to my wife, but Holmes at his most persuasive was hard to refuse.

We heard two sets of footsteps, and Mrs Hudson appeared at the door. 'A young man to see you, sir.' She withdrew, and a slim figure in an ulster stepped forward.

'Thank heavens you're here, Sherlock Holmes.' The face was in shadow from the peak of its hat, but the voice . . . there was something about that voice . . .

'It can't be!' The colour drained from Holmes's face, then came back all at once. 'Irene Adler!'

'Irene Norton now, as you'll recall.' She took off her hat and revealed herself to be just as beautiful as she had been five years before. 'May I sit down?'

'Of course!' Holmes leapt up and pulled a chair forward. 'I thought I would never see you again.' His eyes were as wide and bright as if he had been indulging in one of his stronger stimulants.

'I'm not visiting for a nice little chat, Mr Holmes.' Mrs Norton leaned forward in her chair. 'I need your help. I need it badly. Do you follow the career of our mutual friend, the King of Bohemia?'

'I can scarcely avoid it,' said Holmes. 'He's often in the scandal-sheets.'

'So you'll know that his marriage is in trouble.'

'What does that matter to you?' Holmes regarded his client keenly. 'I thought you had put all that behind you.'

'I have!' she cried. 'The problem is, he hasn't. He has begun to send me letters — such letters! I never reply, and I burn them as soon as I have read them, but now he has given me an ultimatum. If I do not leave my husband and go to him, he will send *that* photograph of us to Godfrey!'

'Mrs Norton, are you telling me that your husband is unaware of your previous relationship with the King?'

'He knows that we had an attachment, of course . . . but not the full extent of it.' Mrs Norton put her head in her hands. 'Godfrey and I thought we were safe. That's why we returned to England; Godfrey wants our children to grow up here. We have lived so quietly that this is the first time I have ventured into London.'

'But why would the photograph cause such trouble? I thought it was a standard portrait of you both.' It took me a moment to recognise Holmes's expression, so rarely had I seen him puzzled.

Her laugh was a mirthless bark. 'You haven't seen what I wrote on the back. It would end our marriage.'

'What *did* you write?'

'I'm not telling you!' she snapped, reddening. 'You'll find out when you get the photograph for me — and I'll pay whatever it takes! I've asked the King, I've begged the King, but he says that he will send it in three days unless I go to him in Bohemia at once . . . ' She rose, and paced the floor.

Sherlock Holmes stood and took her hand in his. 'Mrs Norton, you do not need to pay me. I will do my best to get the photograph back for you. But be warned; I may well fail. There is no point in appealing to the King's better nature; I know that from my previous dealings with him. The only way is to find and steal the photograph. But the King has almost limitless resources, and he is overseas, beyond the reach of my information networks . . . ' Holmes looked away for a moment. 'Would you consider telling your husband about the photograph? Preparing him?'

'No.' Her voice was low but resolute. 'I could not bear it. I would rather die.'

'Well, I will try my hardest. What is the best way to communicate?'

'Wire to my local post office, in the hamlet of Rackham, West Sussex.' Mrs Norton released her hand from his. 'I must leave now for the train. Godfrey thinks I am at a concert. Goodbye, Sherlock Holmes.' She put her hat back on, and the door clicked shut behind her.

Holmes watched her from the window, then pulled the curtain back into place and sighed. 'Watson, I doubt I will succeed in this case. The King is rich, powerful, and unprincipled, and above all, he is not breaking the law.' He sat at the desk, pulled some paper towards him, and began to write; but every few seconds he muttered, and scratched the words out.

'What are you doing, Holmes?' I asked.

'Thinking, Watson. Trying to formulate a strategy. But there is always a block!'

'I need to leave now, too, Holmes,' I said, gently. 'Mary will wonder where I am.'

'Mary? Oh yes . . . ' Holmes smiled. 'Your wife. I always forget.'

'I know.' I patted him on the shoulder, and picked up my hat on the way out.

I was busy for the next few days; my usual round of morning visits was extended into the night by an outbreak of whooping cough. Fortunately my patients, while noisy, were not seriously ill, and a week later I rang the door-bell of 221B Baker Street.

The worry on Billy's face was chased away by a grin as he opened the door. 'I'm glad to see you, sir! The master's acting awful funny. We was thinking of calling a doctor — '

I strode past the boy and made for the stairs. 'What's wrong with him?'

'It came on quite sudden, about twenty minutes ago. I took up the post, and just as I got downstairs I heard 'im laughing. After five minutes I went up to see if he needed anything, but he just waved me away, tears running down his cheeks. And he's still going.' Sure enough, as I climbed the stairs I could hear exhausted gasps, whoops, and giggles.

I rapped on the sitting-room door and entered. 'Holmes, are you all right? What has happened?'

'Everything's all right, Watson,' choked Holmes. 'Here!' He passed me the letter he was holding, and I read:

'Dear Mr Holmes,

I am writing to thank you for your kind assistance. When I received your letter I was unsure what to think. At first I was angry that my wife had taken another man into her confidence. Then I was distressed that Irene had felt the need to do so; that she had thought I would not understand and forgive her actions. And finally I was proud that, as you say, I am a better man than the King of Bohemia.

The package arrived as you suggested it would, in a distinctive pink-tinged wrapping, hand-delivered to my office in Worthing. I weighed it in my hands, and weighed my curiosity to know its contents, and the mind of the man who could do such a deed, against my love for my wife. Then I put it into the fire unopened, and started for home.'

I looked up from the letter with tears in my eyes. 'Holmes, that was a stroke of genius. I had thought you would try to intercept the photograph, or appeal to the King.' I frowned at Holmes, who was still roaring with laughter. 'I don't understand what's so funny. It's rather touching.'

Holmes snorted, and caught his breath. 'Read on, Watson, read on! First I witnessed their marriage, and now this!'

I turned my attention back to the letter, and read:

'Irene was beside herself with joy when I told her what I had done; and throwing her arms around me, she shared some wonderful news. We expect an addition to our family in a few months' time. We would like you to be the child's godfather, and we propose, if he is a boy, to give him the middle name Sherlock. Irene is well, and will write with further news in due course.

Yours sincerely,

Godfrey Norton

PS We intend to continue in our quiet rural life, and would appreciate it if Dr Watson did not chronicle this case, much as we enjoy his contributions to the *Strand Magazine.*'

The Case of the Mysterious Voices

'What can this herald, I wonder?' Holmes mused, on hearing the door-bell ring. 'An exciting new case, I hope.'

'Do you never yearn for the quiet life, Holmes?' I asked. 'Away from the hustle and bustle of London, in a nice villa by the sea . . . '

Holmes shuddered. 'The more hustle the better, as far as I am concerned.'

Billy entered the room followed by a woman who reminded me of a ruffled bird. Her skirts were awry, the feather in her hat draggled, and as she tottered forward she dropped a glove. 'Mrs Pargiter,' announced Billy.

'Madam,' said Holmes, returning her glove with a flourish, 'what can I do for you?'

'Well, Mr Holmes, to be quite honest I'm not sure whether I should speak to you or to Dr Watson.' Mrs

Pargiter's eyes were round and frightened.

'What is the matter, my dear lady?' I said, with my best bedside manner.

She turned to me, her breathing quick and shallow. 'I have been hearing voices, Dr Watson, and I am afraid!'

'All the time?'

'No, doctor, only in the evenings, when I sit in the drawing room after dinner.'

'So you hear no voices now?'

'Only yours, Dr Watson.'

Holmes coughed. 'What do the voices say, Mrs Pargiter?'

'They are indistinct, Mr Holmes. Sometimes I hear a muttered conversation, sometimes there is laughter, as if they are making fun of me. When my husband joins me the voices cease, and he says that I must be imagining it. But I swear on my life, I hear them!' Mrs Pargiter clapped her hand to her heart and let out a sob.

'Mrs Pargiter, Watson and I will call on you tonight, and see if we can get to the root of the problem. Will your husband be at home too?'

'Oh yes,' said Mrs Pargiter, clasping her hands. 'He always joins me after dinner, when he has smoked a pipe.'

*

That evening Mrs Pargiter, pale but composed, received us in her drawing room. 'I will ring for coffee,' she said, rising.

'Can you hear any voices at present?' asked Holmes.

'No, no,' she said. Seconds later, her face took on an expression of the utmost distress. 'Oh! It has begun! They are laughing at me, so horribly!'

I turned to Holmes, whose eyes were wide and staring. 'Good God, man! Can you hear something?'

'Yes,' Holmes whispered, his face a mask of dread. 'I hear it. I hear their mockery. And it is getting louder! No, no!' He jerked this way and that, as if fighting an invisible foe, and in my head I too began to hear faint laughter. Was I imagining it? Was I deluded?

'I will fetch Mr Pargiter!' I cried. 'He needs to bear witness to this!' I rushed to the dining room, flung the door open, and beheld Mr Pargiter sitting at the table with a glass of sherry, and laughing at the conversation issuing from a wooden box in the side cupboard.

'So!' I shouted, pointing at the box. 'What is this infernal device?'

Mr Pargiter had the grace to look embarrassed. 'It is a radio apparatus. Rather an expensive one, which is why I haven't told Mrs P about it.' The conversation gave place to a string quartet. 'It's the very latest thing.'

'It is rather good, actually,' I said. 'What do the buttons do?' Then I recalled the terrified pair next door. 'Mr Pargiter, I fancy you have some explaining to do.'

And so it was that, just once, I, Dr John H. Watson, solved a mystery before Sherlock Holmes.

Sherlock Holmes
and the Burglar

Holmes erupted into the drawing room and flung himself into a chair. 'He's done it again!'

'I presume you mean Fingers Molloy?'

'Who else?' Holmes reached for his violin and scraped a chord which set my teeth on edge.

London had rung with the exploits of mystery man Fingers Molloy for weeks. He had begun by making off with the entire window display of Garrard's the jewellers, replacing it with his calling card. A burglary at Lord Aston's London mansion followed. Both events had taken place at night, but there were no signs of breaking and entering, and all the staff were trusted employees of several years' standing.

'What has he done this time?' I asked.

'Where, you mean. Coutts' Bank!' Holmes ran his

bow across the strings of his violin again, making a marginally pleasanter sound.

'Oh, I say! What did he take this time?'

'He took all the money in the tills, and left his card in each one. They can count themselves lucky that he did not touch the safe.'

'And no one knows how he got in?'

'No. No forced locks, no broken windows.'

'That's impossible!' I cried. 'Three burglaries of secure establishments, and not a trace except for his card!'

'Watson, it cannot be impossible! It is just that I have not worked out his method yet.' He lit his pipe and retreated behind a fug of smoke, while I resumed reading my novel.

'If you could steal anything in London, Watson, what would you choose?' Holmes was looking at me thoughtfully.

I put my book down and considered. 'I would take money; sovereigns, as banknotes can be traced. But Fingers Molloy enjoys making a show of his work. I imagine his next choice will be something valuable, securely kept, and in a prominent location.'

'Bravo, Watson!' cried Holmes. 'You are a criminal mastermind! Hurry, we have no time to lose!'

'But where are we going?'

'To wait for Fingers Molloy to arrive for his next crime, the theft of the Crown Jewels!'

I stifled another yawn. 'Holmes, the jewel house is about to close. Please can we go home now?' I gestured towards the decrepit cleaning woman moving round the glass cases with her trolley.

Holmes sighed theatrically. 'Perhaps you are right. We will come back tomorrow.' As we left Holmes put his finger to his lips and steered me towards a curtained alcove.

'What are we doing?' I whispered.

'Waiting.'

A few minutes later the door of the Jewel House creaked open. We heard the cleaning woman's shuffle and the squeaky wheels of her trolley. Holmes sprang from behind the curtain and wrestled her to the ground.

'Holmes, have you gone mad?' I cried, untangling myself from the curtain. Then I noticed that the cleaning woman was wearing trousers under her dress, and her grey hair was lying a few feet away.

'Watson, allow me to introduce Fingers Molloy! Come on, give me a hand!' Holmes called, setting his knee on the man's chest. 'You'll find some standard-issue cuffs in my pocket.' I snapped them on, and Fingers Molloy ceased struggling.

'I'll have you for false imprisonment, Sherlock Holmes!'

Holmes frowned. 'How do you know my name? We've never met.'

37

A slow smile spread over Fingers Molloy's weaselly face. 'Oh, we have. Just not yet. Anyway, you can't lock me up, mate. Impersonating a woman is no crime.'

'No, Fingers, but stealing a crown is.' Holmes strolled over to the trolley and pulled away a bundle of cloths to reveal St Edward's Crown nestling in a bucket. 'Now then, I heard no breaking glass in there. Care to tell me how you did it, Fingers, in exchange for a reduced sentence?'

Fingers thought it over for a minute. 'May as well,' he said, grinning. 'You'll like this, Mr Holmes. Pull that big cloth off the trolley.'

Holmes did so, and whistled as a metal box covered in dials and levers was revealed. The biggest dial bore the inscription 'Time', and a range of options from five minutes to five years.

'So you can travel in time with this contraption?'

'Yessir,' said Fingers, sitting up. 'Courtesy of a scientist friend of mine. It's really easy to use. You just set the dial and grab the two wires and off you go.'

My brow furrowed as I tried to make sense of it. 'So you've been going into the near future, stealing things, and bringing them back with you into the present?'

'That's it,' said Fingers. 'The perfect crime, you might say. All the broken glass and forced locks never come back with you.'

Holmes turned the dial to 6 MONTHS. 'I imagine your sentence will be a bit heavier than that, Fingers,' he smiled.

'Careful, Holmes,' I muttered. 'You can't trust a crook.'

Holmes turned round. 'I know what I'm —' Fingers launched himself at the time machine, cuffed hands reaching for the wires.

'No!' shouted Holmes, and lunged after the thief. He only succeeded in knocking the bucket to the floor as Fingers Molloy, time machine, trolley and all, vanished into thin air.

We looked at each other. 'What do we do now?' I said, bemused.

Holmes picked up St Edward's Crown from the floor. 'Take this to Scotland Yard for safekeeping, I suppose.' He wrapped it in one of Fingers Molloy's cleaning cloths. 'I have no idea how we'll explain it, though. Come on, let's get a cab.'

The fresh evening breeze did nothing to clear my head. 'Won't we tell them the truth, Holmes?'

'Who would believe us?' Holmes shrugged. 'A burglar who uses a time machine? I would be a laughing-stock! But wait — Watson, make a note! Today's date, and . . .' — he consulted his watch — 'five minutes to five. Write it down, man, quick! We'll come back for him in six months' time!'

'So time is on our side!' I chuckled, as I closed my notebook. A young man with a book under his arm had stopped a few feet away and was staring straight at us.

He opened the book — Huxley's *Physiography*, I noted — and scribbled something on the flyleaf. Then he hurried on down the street until he was invisible in the shadows.

The Case of the Severed Hand

'The criminals of today have lost their verve,' complained Holmes, filling his pipe. 'Where is the great mastermind, the schemer, the Machiavelli?' He stuck the pipe in his mouth and fumbled for a match.

The door-bell pealed once, gently. 'Maybe that's him now,' I remarked.

'I doubt it,' Holmes sighed.

'Mrs Florence Buckminster,' Billy announced. A soberly-dressed lady in her thirties, carrying a wicker basket, stepped forward.

'Do take a seat.' Holmes waved a hand towards the armchair. 'May Billy take your basket?'

'No, no, I'll hold on to it, thank you,' said Mrs Buckminster, putting it at her feet as if it were a live bomb.

'Mrs Buckminster, I will come to the point,' said Holmes. 'You appear agitated, and this is related to the contents of your basket.'

'I don't know what to do, Mr Holmes!' she wailed. 'I'm terrible at puzzles!'

'Watson, pour a large brandy for the lady,' Holmes ordered. 'Shall we start from the beginning, Mrs Buckminster?'

'Yes, please,' she gulped, wiping her eyes with a lace-edged handkerchief. 'It began a fortnight ago, when a parcel was delivered to me containing — this!' She lifted the cover of the basket to reveal a human hand packed in straw.

'Good Lord!' I cried.

Holmes stared at the hand, and loosened his necktie. 'I should like a drink of water, Watson, if you don't mind. Quite stuffy in here.'

Mrs Buckminster giggled. 'It's not a real one!' She picked the hand up and held it out to Holmes, who recoiled. 'It's made of wax,' she said, and replaced it in the basket. 'I never thought it was real.'

'Why not, madam?' I asked. 'It's very lifelike.'

'Yes,' said Mrs Buckminster. 'It's mine — see?' She put her hand beside the one in the basket, and they were indeed identical, down to a little mole at the base of the thumb.

Holmes wiped his brow. 'So someone sent you a model of your hand.'

'That's right. And there was a note with it which said, "Guess a letter, and leave this note under the doormat."

So I wrote an S on the paper, and put it under the mat, and two days later, the other hand came!'

'No!' Holmes began to pace. 'Mrs Buckminster, I must congratulate you on your calmness in the face of such a sinister crime.'

'Well, not really,' said Mrs Buckminster. 'I used to be an artist's model before I met Mr Buckminster, and I posed for a shop mannequin too. Whoever's doing this has got one of me, and is sending it bit by bit.'

'Was there a note with the second hand?' asked Holmes.

'Oh yes,' said Mrs Buckminster. 'It was the same note, but it had a gallows drawn on it, and they'd written, "Wrong! Guess again."'

'Hangman!' Holmes cried. 'So how far has the game progressed?'

Mrs Buckminster trembled. 'They sent my second leg yesterday. And the note said, "We will deliver further parcels to your husband, unless you leave a thousand pounds under the mat."'

'I take it Mr Buckminster is unaware of your past,' Holmes said gently.

'Of course he is! And the head's exactly like me! And I don't have a thousand pounds!' Mrs Buckminster wrung her hands.

'Do you have the latest note with you?' Mrs Buckminster fumbled in the basket and passed a crumpled sheet to Holmes. He picked up a magnifying glass from the bureau and examined it. 'Hmm. Do you have any enemies, Mrs Buckminster?'

'No, not at all. I left my former life behind when I met Mr Buckminster.'

'Ah.' Holmes peered at the note again. 'So, you have guessed N, R and I correctly, but S, E, B, L and D are wrong.' He showed me the sequence, which read as follows:

$$\_\,N\,\_\,\_\,R\,\_\,\_\,\_\,\_\,\_\,R\,\_\,\_\,I\,\_$$

I scratched my head. 'I can make neither head nor tail of it.'

'Anthropomorphic!' said Holmes, writing the missing letters in. 'Ha! Our blackmailer has a sense of humour.' He handed the note back to Mrs Buckminster. 'Place this under your doormat as usual, and Watson and I will watch for the perpetrator tonight. As he has not been caught on your doorstep, I suspect he visits under cover of darkness.'

Holmes was proved right. After no more than five hours spent shivering in Montagu Square gardens, we observed a figure emerge from a side street, look around, then dart straight for Mrs Buckminster's door. 'Now!' yelled Holmes, bursting out of the shrubbery and grabbing the figure's arm. 'Monsieur Petit, you had better explain yourself.'

'I require the money to shape and manufacture a new mannequin,' M. Petit said, shaking Holmes off and adjusting his sleeve. 'Madame's shape is out of fashion now. The shops want a model smaller *here* and bigger *here*.' He indicated approximate measurements with his hands.

'That is neither here nor there,' admonished Holmes. 'You will cease this despicable business, and find a loan by legitimate means. Now be off with you!' M. Petit scurried away into the shadows.

'How did you know it was him?' I asked, as we strolled along Oxford Street.

'Elementary, Watson,' said Holmes. 'The hand we saw was in pristine condition, and had clearly never been used in a shop display. The most obvious source was the mannequin maker, and some brief enquiries in Harrod's elicited the information I needed. Now, I fancy that if we proceed to Covent Garden Market we can procure an early breakfast. Would you care to join me?'

A Case of Stage Fright

'Telegram, sir,' said Billy, handing it over. 'From the Lyceum.'

'What is it now?' muttered Holmes. 'Perhaps this time Irving wants to know where I buy my deerstalkers.'

At first Holmes, and I as his chronicler, were flattered when Henry Irving had asked whether he might stage a production of *The Speckled Band*, one of Holmes's most famous cases. However, we had answered so many enquiries and requests that I never wanted to hear the words 'speckled', 'snake', or 'actors' ever again.

'Why can't they just read the book?' I grumbled. 'It's all in there.'

'Need help stage fright threatens whole production come immediately,' Holmes read. 'I'm a consulting detective, not an acting coach!' He screwed up the telegram and threw it into the fire, then sighed. 'The difficulty is that if the play is ridiculous, it might harm my — our — reputation. Come on, Watson, let's stroll down.'

The foyer of the theatre was deserted, except for an anxious-looking man examining some playbills. 'Oh Mr Holmes, thank heavens you're here,' he cried, with a faint trace of brogue. 'I'm at my wits' end!'

'So I see from the telegram,' Holmes remarked. 'But what makes you think I can help, Mr . . . '

'Stoker, Bram Stoker,' the man said, extending a hand. 'I'm the manager here. I engaged a talented young actress, Sybil Marshall, to play the female lead. Now, in the last week of rehearsals, she freezes, stammers a few incoherent words, and runs off-stage. And we open on Friday!'

Holmes raised his eyebrows. 'Could you use the understudy?'

Stoker shook his head. 'You haven't seen her act. We tried a run-through with her and it played as a comedy.'

'Oh dear.' Holmes's mouth twitched. 'What does Miss Marshall say when this fit comes upon her?'

'"The eyes, the terrible eyes! It is the speckled band!"' Stoker quavered.

'That sounds rather good,' I commented.

'Not when it's the first scene, it isn't.'

'I see,' said Holmes. 'When is your next rehearsal?'

'Tonight,' Stoker winced. 'The dress rehearsal.'

'Then I shall visit tonight, in secret, and view this

phenomenon with my own eyes.'

A radiant smile spread over Mr Stoker's countenance. 'Thank you, Mr Holmes! If anyone can solve this mystery, it is you.' He pumped Holmes's hand until the great detective managed to disengage himself and exit, stage left.

*

'Aren't you rather overdressed, Holmes?' I asked as we approached the stage door of the Lyceum that evening.

'This old thing?' said Holmes, swirling his opera cloak about him. 'It is very useful for concealment in cases such as this.'

Stoker welcomed us with whispered effusiveness and directed us to a box with an excellent view of the stage, one side of the wings, and the house. Once the lights went down, we took our seats and prepared to enjoy the show. I thought that the actor playing Holmes was good, but rather mannered in his delivery. Watson, though, came across as extremely stupid, and I determined to inform Mr Stoker of this error later.

When Miss Marshall appeared Holmes and I sat up. Stoker was right. She appeared uneasy, and not three minutes in, she pointed into the darkness, and shrieked 'The eyes! The speckled band!'

A second later, Holmes cried 'The eyes!' and bounded onto the balcony. The lights went up just as Holmes leapt into the stalls, his cloak billowing about him. He raced to the back of the theatre, looking around wildly. 'Aha!' Holmes reached under the seats and extracted a young lady in an identical costume to Miss Marshall's. 'Your understudy, I presume — and behold! The eyes, the terrible eyes!' He held up a lantern covered save for two eye-shaped points of light. 'Ingenious, I must say.'

'Bertha!' Sybil Marshall gasped. The understudy, now looking as terrified as Miss Marshall had done, made a hasty exit via the back door.

'I fancy that your stage-fright is now at an end, Miss Marshall.' Holmes declaimed. 'We will bid you farewell, and let you continue with your rehearsal.'

Mr Stoker led the cast in applause. 'Mr Holmes, what a performance! I cannot thank you enough. The way you leapt from the balcony! It was like . . . like . . . ' He gasped, pulled a notebook from his pocket, and became so absorbed in his memorandum that he barely noticed our departure, despite Holmes's rather melodramatic cloak-swirling.

As a thank-you gesture, Mr Stoker sent us dress circle tickets for the opening night of *The Speckled Band*. Miss Marshall was superb, and the play was a resounding success. Personally, I felt that the dream sequence with the dancing girls was an unnecessary distraction from the plot, but I sense that I was in the minority.

The Case of the Missing Elephant

It was a day like any other at 221B Baker Street. Holmes sawed at the strings of his violin, deep in thought, while I, rendered blissfully immune to Holmes's din by my patent earplugs, read the latest *Strand Magazine*. Thus we heard nothing until the door burst open, flung wide by a red-faced, scowling Mrs Hudson. I snatched out my earplugs, and Holmes paused in his cacophony.

'Mr Topper,' bawled Mrs Hudson, and withdrew.

Holmes pointed his bow at Mr Topper. 'From your brass buttons and your peaked cap, I deduce that you are a public servant of some kind.'

Mr Topper stepped forward and swallowed. 'That's right, sir, I — '

Holmes wrinkled his nose. Indeed, the advancing

man was accompanied by a loathsome smell. 'Lavatory attendant?'

'Er, no, sir. I am the head keeper at the Zoological Gardens, in Regent's Park.'

'Just as I thought!' Holmes exclaimed. 'And what brings you here, my good man?'

Mr Topper's words came out in a rush. 'The pride of our zoo has gone missing, sir! Our Indian elephant, Maharajah, has disappeared from his enclosure!'

Holmes sat bolt upright. 'Are there any traces of forced entry?'

'No, nothing at all.' Mr Topper began to sniffle. 'He was such a lovely, gentle pachyderm . . . '

'There, there,' soothed Holmes. 'We will find your elephant, never fear.' He sprang to his feet, swapped his violin for a deerstalker and magnifying glass, and motioned to me to follow.

At the zoo we were obstructed by two university students shaking buckets in our faces. 'Money for Rag Week, sir!' Holmes waved them aside irritably, and strode to the unoccupied elephant house.

Mr Topper and I watched from the path as Holmes turned straw, peered into corners, and tested locks. 'You are right, Mr Topper. An elephant has vanished and left no trace. This is indeed a worthy mystery.'

'*He's* not an elephant!' shouted a pointing small girl, and began to wail. Holmes climbed out and stood with us, nonplussed and sheepish, as the child's nanny led her away through the crowd. Then a piercing trumpet cut through the hubbub like a knife through butter. Holmes and I exchanged glances and rushed towards the entrance, with the keeper in hot pursuit.

The Rag Week Parade was approaching. At the head of it, ridden by a crew of students in white coats, stethoscopes and top hats, was a disgruntled-looking elephant.

'Is that him?' Holmes asked Mr Topper.

'Maharajah!' breathed Mr Topper, his face suffused with joy. He rushed towards the elephant, who halted, grasped the keeper round the waist with his trunk, and plonked him on his back. The crowd cheered. Mr Topper doffed his cap, bowed and patted Maharajah, who trumpeted.

Holmes reached up and grabbed the ankle of the nearest student, who appeared rather seasick. 'Care to explain?'

The student swallowed. 'We thought it would be a good stunt to get an elephant for the Rag Week Parade, so we bribed one of the night keepers to let us borrow him for the day. We were going to give him back, honest! See how much money we've raised!' He thrust his bucket, brimming with coins, under Holmes's nose.

Holmes promptly swiped the bucket. '*This* is the elephant rental fee. Get down right away and we won't press charges.' The young man nodded and, with a whistle to his friends, slid down Maharajah's tail.

'I think this will do, Mr Topper,' Holmes shouted, rattling the bucket. 'Case closed.'

A Bottle of Distilled Water

'It is no use, Holmes,' I chuckled. 'I have known you for many years now, and I can read you like a book.'

Holmes glanced up from the network of chemical apparatus he was assembling. 'Perhaps you are right about that, Watson. However, I maintain that my new test will provide a foolproof method of detecting strychnine poisoning, once it is ready. Surely that is worth some approbation?'

I laughed aloud. 'Of course, Holmes, of course.'

Holmes crossed to his store of chemicals, then exclaimed in dismay, 'I have almost run out of distilled water!' He ran a hand through his hair. 'Just at the most delicate stage, too . . . '

'I can go and get some, Holmes,' I said, feeling rather guilty that I had poked fun at my companion.

'Oh Watson, that would be a boon.' Holmes retreated behind his equipment, then poked his head out again. 'Would you mind getting it from Jones the druggist, on Delancey Street? I trust him in these matters.'

'Very well,' I said, relishing the prospect of a walk across the park on such a fine April morning. Holmes did not reply, already absorbed in making minute adjustments to his setup.

I enjoyed my stroll in Regent's Park, taking the opportunity to indulge in some people-watching. *You are not the only student of the human condition, Holmes,* I thought. Delancey Street was a short step from Gloucester Gate, and Jones had an ample supply of distilled water in stock. I purchased a bottle and took my leave, imbued with a pleasant sense that I would pour oil on troubled waters.

As I approached the park an old woman with a basket accosted me. 'That stuff'll do you no good, dearie,' she said, wagging a wool-clad finger at my bottle of distilled water. 'You need Elphinstone's Patent Elixir, and lucky for you I have one bottle left.' She raised the cover of her basket and thrust a bottle of viscous mustard-coloured liquid at me.

'I don't think I do,' I said, quickening my pace.

She cackled. 'You should try it. I can see you suffer from aches and pains, and it's a true miracle worker. The Elixir would clear up that bad leg of yours. And that troublesome shoulder.'

'No thank you!' I cried, running for the sanctuary of

the park.

'Suit yourself!' she bellowed after me.

Once through the park gates I slowed down, looking behind me occasionally for the elderly harridan, and after a few minutes the healing power of fresh air and sunshine began its work upon me.

'*Hoy!* You in the bowler, with the gin bottle! What do you think you're up to?'

A plump, uniformed figure marched towards me, moustache bristling, and jabbed me in the chest. 'This is a public park, not a public house!' he shouted.

I stepped back, and drew myself up to my full height. 'This is distilled water,' I said, holding the bottle out. 'Can't you read?'

'I am the park-keeper, and no-one speaks to me like that!' He puffed himself up until he resembled a red-faced, brass-buttoned toad. 'Get out! And keep off the grass while you're at it!'

'I am leaving, anyway,' I said, huffily.

'Yes, you are!' said the park-keeper, and charged at me with a noise like a bull letting off steam. I am not ashamed to admit that I took to my heels and cut across the lawn. That, however, was a tactical error, as the damp ground coated my shoes in mud. I retreated to the path, but the damage was done.

'Oi!' a voice shouted as I passed through the gate nearest Baker Street. '*Look* at them shoes! Sixpence and I'll clean 'em for yer!' The voice came from a dirty, cheery fellow in shirtsleeves, sitting cross-legged behind a wooden box. 'C'mon!' He flapped his rag at me.

I reflected that going back to Baker Street with my shoes covered in mud would lead to questions, and doubtless ridicule. 'All right, my man.' I walked over and put my foot on the box, and the bootblack set to work, whistling an air popular with the local organ grinders.

'Going anywhere nice for yer 'olidays this summer, sir?'

'Er, no, I have nothing planned.' I said to his flat cap.

The bootblack tutted. 'That's a shame. Still, you'll be in London for the Jubilee, that'll be a sight to see. Fifty years on the throne! There'll be bunting everywhere, an' a special coin, and who knows what flummery. Other foot now, sir.'

I obliged. 'What's that bottle you're carrying, sir? Liquor?' The bootblack squinted up at me.

'Distilled water,' I said firmly, determined not to start any more disputes.

'Well, now. An' what do you do with that?'

'Experiments.'

'Oh, so you're a *scientist*,' the bootblack told my left foot. 'What sort of experiments?'

'It's for a friend.'

The bootblack looked up at me again, but all his cheer had vanished. 'I reckon that stuff's yours. Secret experiments, eh?' The eyes narrowed. 'I 'ope you're not blowing things up, now . . . '

'I told you, it's for a friend. I'm not a scientist, I'm a doctor.'

'A doctor.' The bootblack snorted. 'Course you are.' He gave my shoe a last swipe with his rag and held out his hand. 'Sixpence, please.' I slapped the coin into it and stalked away.

I arrived back at 221B feeling as if I had run the gauntlet. I resolved to give Holmes his water and then read in my room. But as I ascended Mrs Hudson appeared and insisted on my opinion of a leg of lamb which 'smelt funny'. I only escaped by swearing that I would be happy to eat it so long as it was not crawling with maggots, and no doubt Holmes would be too.

I arrived upstairs to find Holmes quite cheered in spirits, watching purple liquid drip through his glass pipes into a flask. 'Watson!' he exclaimed. 'I had almost given you up for lost. Did you have to wait at the druggist's?'

'No,' I said, putting the bottle on the sideboard. I assumed my slippers, poured myself a stiff brandy, and plopped onto the sofa.

'Then what happened?' Holmes asked, eyebrows raised. 'I heard Mrs Hudson buttonhole you, but that was only a few minutes.'

'It's a long story,' I said, taking a gulp of brandy.

Holmes examined my discarded shoes. 'Hmm. These are clean . . . suspiciously clean, but there is fresh mud in the sole, particularly at the heels. I suspect you of running around in the park, Watson, and getting your shoes cleaned afterwards to hide it.' He laughed and made a tiny adjustment to his experiment.

'You don't know the half of it,' I said. 'I'll take those to my room, if you don't mind.' I picked up my shoes and tucked the newspaper under my arm.

'Wait!' Holmes's voice was full of concern. 'You're limping, Watson.'

'Probably the weather,' I said, and opened the door.

'Won't you try some of this? I believe it's rather good.'

I stared at the bottle Holmes held out to me. Elphinstone's Patent Elixir! 'What the — ?'

'I do apologise, Watson,' chuckled Holmes. 'I have been working on a few new personae lately, as brother Mycroft tells me that various criminals are targeting the Jubilee. When you said earlier that you could read me like a book — well, it inspired me to try one of my new characters out.'

'That female quack outside the druggist's was you?'

Holmes hung his head. 'I am afraid so.'

I sighed in exasperation. 'Holmes, if you hadn't been so persistent I wouldn't have upset the park-keeper. I won't be able to show myself in the park for a week . . . '

Holmes giggled.

'It's not funny!' I cried.

'Dangerous stuff, that distilled water . . . ' Holmes managed to choke out.

'You again!' I shouted.

'Good job you managed to get your shoes clean!' Holmes burbled, holding up sixpence.

'I — oh, for heaven's sake! Was this whole trip a fool's errand?'

Holmes patted my shoulder. 'My dear Watson, not at all. I did need the distilled water, though not urgently; and I also needed to make sure my disguises would allow me to traverse London unrecognised. Who better to test them than my dear friend Watson, who knows me best of all?'

'Perhaps,' I said, slightly mollified, 'but being the subject of your experiments is hard work.'

'Then let us take the rest of the day off.' Holmes extinguished his Bunsen burner. 'I will ask Mrs Hudson to put us up a picnic, and we will laze in the sunshine with no fear of the park-keeper.'

'Holmes . . . '

'Yes, Watson?'

'Mrs Hudson and the leg of lamb . . . that wasn't you as well, was it?'

Holmes smiled and shook his head. 'No, Watson. While I am happy to assume various characters in the line of duty, I would not presume to attempt Mrs Hudson. Indeed, I would declare our landlady inimitable. Cucumber sandwiches for the picnic, Watson?'

'Yes please, Holmes.'

The Case of the Incriminating Footprint

'Have you formed an opinion yet, Holmes?' I shouted above the rattling wheels of the brougham.

Holmes shook his head. 'The telegram says so little that it would be unwise.' We were travelling to the sleepy village of Addington, summoned from our beds by a wire from the Inspector: 'Duel come at once meet Pelican Inn Addington Lestrade'.

The carriage slowed. 'I imagine we are about to find out more,' said Holmes, jumping down with characteristic energy.

A policeman standing outside the inn doffed his hat. 'Sergeant Ribstock, sir, at your service. The Inspector has asked me to escort you to the crime scene while he takes some statements in the village.'

The officer took us along the village street, through

the churchyard, and into the field beyond. 'This is where the event took place, between six and seven o'clock this morning. The injured party, Mr Robert Hampson, is a businessman well-known locally. He was seriously wounded, and has been conveyed to the nearest hospital. He would not reveal his opponent's identity, only murmuring weakly that honour had been satisfied.'

'What of the seconds?' Holmes asked.

'There were none,' the policeman replied. 'Mr Hampson dragged himself to the church. Luckily the door was unlocked, and he managed to ring one of the church bells to call for help.'

Holmes peered at the flattened grass beside us. 'I thought as much . . . would you be so kind as to show me the underside of your boot, Sergeant Ribstock?' The Sergeant complied, with a hop or two. 'As I would expect, the regulation model.' Then he stiffened like a hound on the scent. 'Aha!' He pulled out his magnifying glass, knelt in the mud, then lay prostrate, scanning the ground for a full three minutes before rising and dusting himself down.

'Well, Sergeant Ribstock, I can give only a few details about the assailant. He is a heavy-footed but active and vigorous man of around forty, who favours the right leg. He is a man of modest means, an economical, even miserly man, who visited Paris between three and five years ago. He smoked a cheroot standing here. After the duel he appears to have walked towards his opponent. However, he offered no assistance, but strolled around the field for some time, perhaps debating what action to take, before walking back into the churchyard and thence making his escape.'

'Wonderful!' I exclaimed. Holmes smiled modestly.

Sergeant Ribstock finished writing in his notebook and looked up. 'Ah, here comes Inspector Lestrade.' Holmes waved to the rapidly approaching figure of the Inspector, who waved back. But when the Inspector had almost reached us Holmes let out a howl and stabbed an accusing finger at the inspector's feet.

'Lestrade, when will you stop trampling all over crime scenes? I have muddied my knees for nothing!' He seized the Inspector's leg and lifted it to display a worn-down but unmistakably French-made boot.

'Ow!' the Inspector shrieked, wobbling. He grabbed at Holmes to steady himself and the pair tumbled into the mud.

'Oh dear.' Sergeant Ribstock snapped his notebook closed, 'Let us hope that the injured gentleman turns informer, for I suspect that is our best chance at a solution. Dr Watson, if you would welcome a glass of beer at the inn before travelling back to London, I should be glad to accommodate you.'

The Case of the Disappearing Irregular

'I cannot wait for the nights to draw in,' remarked Holmes, listlessly scraping the bow across his violin.

'If that's the noise you plan to make while you're waiting, neither can I,' I winced.

'London's no fun in the summer,' Holmes declared. 'The sun lights up all the dark corners. But hark, the door-bell. Perhaps a criminal has found a lurking-place after all.'

We listened as Billy answered the door. The conversation escalated to an outraged bellow, and Holmes and I stepped into the hall to find a mob of Baker Street Irregulars sitting on Billy's head.

'Sorry, Mr H,' said the largest lad, getting up. 'He wouldn't let us come in.'

'You go round to the back door, Smiffy!' Billy

mumbled into the carpet, and an Irregular pinned him a little more firmly.

'Not today. We're here on business.'

'Really?' Holmes hooked his thumbs into his waistcoat pockets. 'Do tell.'

Smiffy looked all around, then hissed, 'Wiggins has vanished!'

'Wiggins?' I asked.

'Yes, the leader of the Irregulars,' snapped Holmes. 'Do pay attention, Watson.'

'We're like a rudderless ship wivout 'im.' Smiffy began to sniff.

'Oh, for heaven's sake!' Holmes whipped out his handkerchief and thrust it at Smiffy. 'Weeping won't help. How long has Wiggins been gone?'

'Two days, sir. We woke up under the arch, just as usual, and he wasn't there.'

'Do you think someone has taken him?' Holmes began to pace up and down the hall.

'Ooh no, sir,' piped a little voice from the region of Billy's middle. 'Wiggins would've put up a fight. He was so brave and strong . . . aaooowww!' Several of the smaller Irregulars began to bawl.

'Did Wiggins act any differently before he disappeared?'

Smiffy considered. 'He was begging just as usual, mos'ly. But there was an incident a few days ago — '

'What sort of incident?' Holmes interrupted.

'We was standing about, mindin' our own biz, when a young girl went by and her handkerchief fell on the ground. Wiggins went to pick it up, and out of nowhere she clouted him round the 'ead. He just stood there, dazed-like, while she gave him a mouthful. Teased him something rotten, we did.'

'What sort of girl was she?' asked Holmes.

Smiffy scratched his head. 'Hard to say, sir. She was maybe sixteen, and dressed nice, but her langwidge — !'

'And that was the only unusual thing that happened?'

'Well . . . the day before he disappeared, we was watching the world go by an' a carriage pulled up opposite, an' he stared at it like he'd seen a ghost — or no, pleased he was, like it was a nice ghost. We asked him what he was gawking at, but he wouldn't say.'

'What did the carriage look like? Was it a private carriage?'

'Oh yes, it had a coat of arms on the side. A green dragon on a yellow shield.'

Holmes thought for a moment, then smiled. 'Watson, we will take a short trip into the country. Smiffy, I will report back on my return.'

'Where are we going, Holmes?' I asked, as the train rattled along.

'Berkshire, to the country seat of Sir Richard Bevis, whose coat of arms matches Smiffy's description. I wonder what we shall find there,' Holmes mused.

From the station we took a cab, and half an hour

later Holmes and I trudged up the gravel drive of Bevis Hall. Holmes rang the bell, and within seconds a cheery pageboy opened the door. 'Wot can I do for you?' he grinned.

'I would like to speak to Sir Richard, if he is at home. Here is my card,' Holmes said, holding it out.

The page's face fell. 'You don't know me?'

Holmes's jaw dropped. 'Wiggins?'

'Large as life, sah!'

'I didn't recognise you without your usual layer of grime,' Holmes laughed.

'I miss it,' said Wiggins, shining a button with his sleeve, 'but cleanliness goes wiv the job.'

'So what are you doing here?' I asked.

'I was drawn here by destiny,' Wiggins murmured. 'The love of my life whacked me on the 'ead, and the very next day I saw her in the carriage. I clocked the coat of arms, and I knew I 'ad to foller. So I 'itched a ride or two, and turned up here, at the back door. Lucky for me they'd sacked the pageboy for pilferin', so they took me on 'cos of my honest face.'

'And who is the love of your life, exactly?'

'Gertie? She's the lady's maid,' Wiggins said fondly. 'She's already warmin' to me. I said hello to her this morning and she didn't swear once.'

'Well, at least Wiggins is safe,' I said, as we walked down the drive to the waiting cab.

'True,' said Holmes, 'although I suspect he will tire of

his gilded cage and return to Baker Street before too long. You can take the boy out of London, but you can't take London out of the boy.' He leapt into the cab. 'Come along, Watson.'

The Master of Deduction

'I maintain, Watson, that any half-decent detective can deduce a great deal about their client before they have even opened their mouth.'

Holmes was in belligerent mood, and I had witnessed too many astonishing displays of his observational faculty to disagree. However, I couldn't resist inciting him to another demonstration. 'Holmes, I challenge you to sum up our next visitor before they have uttered a word.'

Holmes's eyes narrowed. 'Very well! We shall see . . .' A ring at the bell interrupted him. 'Ha! The game is afoot!' He sprang up and I followed, determined to ensure fair play.

Our visitor was a lady of middle age, respectably-dressed, and somewhat flustered. 'Dear lady,' said Holmes, 'do take a seat. Would you be so kind as to allow me a few moments' grace before I enquire your business, as I am engaged in a speculation with my good friend Dr Watson.'

She nodded, eyes wide, hands twisting her grey gloves.

Holmes looked her up and down. 'We have here a lady of some breeding who has fallen on hard times. Observe the hat, of good quality but now out of fashion and with signs of wear which the owner has done her best to disguise. However, the lady's hands are well-kept and unused to hard work. The lady's manner suggests she has come here about a matter both distressing and personal; I suspect a matter of the heart. Her obvious embarrassment suggests a straying or even vanished husband, possibly under circumstances she is loth to reveal.'

Our visitor bit her lip, and appeared to quiver. Holmes put a soothing hand on her arm. 'Do not worry, madam, we will take good care of you and do our utmost to solve your case.' He shot me a triumphant glance. 'Have I approached the truth?'

The lady burst out laughing. 'What a load of tosh!' she cried, with a distinct Cockney twang. 'I'm in my Sunday best, and I bought the whole outfit for sixpence at a church fundraiser!'

Holmes gasped. 'But — your hands!'

She smiled indulgently. 'I work on the accessories counter in Dickins and Jones. I have to keep my hands nice because they're on show all the time.'

'Well, why have you come to see us?' asked Holmes, nettled. 'Am I right about that?'

She grinned. 'No! I wanted to see how Billy was getting on.'

'Billy?'

'Yes, Billy, your pageboy. I'm his mother. Where is he, anyway? I expected him to answer the door.'

'Well, I'm not entirely sure . . . ' said Holmes, looking around as if Billy might be on the window-ledge or in the bookcase.

Billy's mother howled with laughter. 'To think I was nervous about meeting the great Sherlock Holmes! Call yourself a detective? You don't even know where your servants are!' She rose. 'I'll come back later, when your housekeeper's in.'

As we watched her walk down the street, still laughing, Holmes muttered 'That, Watson, was the exception which proves the rule. I'd be grateful if you didn't record this case for posterity.'

The Mystery of Mornington Crescent

I pick up my pen to record this case knowing that it will never venture outside the pages of this notebook. However, I have made a commitment to document every case of Sherlock Holmes's which I attend, and I will not shirk this even when the account is available only to ourselves.

It was the purest coincidence that I became involved in the case at all. My practice had grown so busy that I rarely saw Holmes, who had retired from practice and moved to Sussex. Indeed, the London traffic meant that seeing my own patients was difficult enough. I increasingly resorted to the Underground Electric Railways to shuttle between different neighbourhoods, emerging into daylight blinking like a mole with a doctor's bag.

On the day in question I broke ground at Baker Street with the aim of strolling down Memory Lane and perhaps even dropping in on Mrs Hudson for a cup of tea. I chuckled as I climbed the Underground stairs, remembering one of Holmes's pleasanter cases, and when I heard the familiar 'Hullo, Watson!' I thought that I must be dreaming.

'Holmes! What brings you here?' I clapped him on the back.

'I am asking myself the same question,' Holmes laughed. 'Watson, I am glad to see you! Firstly because it is always a pleasure, and secondly because you are clearly conversant with the underground train system.'

I bowed slightly. 'I would be delighted to assist, Holmes. What is your destination?'

'Mornington Crescent.'

'Ah.' I pulled out my pocket-map. 'Well, first of all you take a Metropolitan Line train to Gower Street — no, Gower Street doesn't link to the Hampstead Railway, so you go on to King's Cross. From there you take a City and South London Railway train to Euston, and then one stop on the Hampstead Railway to Mornington Crescent.'

'How streamlined.' Holmes brushed a speck of dust from his lapel.

'I admit it's a little convoluted. You get used to it, though.' I checked the map again. 'Oh dear . . . '

'What?' called Holmes, who had begun to descend.

'The train doesn't stop at Mornington Crescent for an hour. We can probably walk there in half the time.'

Holmes snorted, and climbed back up. 'Give me a cab any day.'

Walking the streets of London together was almost like old times. Holmes enquired after my wife and my practice, and I enquired after his business in London. 'Well, as you know, Watson, I only retired because the criminals had grown so dull,' Holmes laughed. 'When I received a letter from the man we are meeting today, I almost jumped for joy. You know how I hate to be bored.' I nodded, recalling Holmes's fits of ennui, which had invariably led to discordant violin-playing, chemical experimentation, and target practice on the sprigged wallpaper.

As we approached the handsome maroon facade of the station, I noticed a man standing outside, glancing around in a restless manner. He was perhaps thirty-five, of medium height and build, and while his clothes were ordinary he was uncommonly neat. He spied us and hurried forward.

'Mr Holmes!' he cried, pumping Holmes's hand.

'That is correct,' said Holmes, wincing slightly. 'Jabez Hope, I presume. Do tell your boss that purchasing a more modern typewriter will save time and money in the long run.'

Mr Hope stared. 'How on earth — ?'

'Oh, it is simple,' said Holmes. 'I see that your fingers

are stained with ink. These are not the irregular stains or smudges from a leaking pen, but the precise line which indicates a typewriter ribbon. As the rest of your appearance is immaculate, I assume that the machine is at fault. The other clue was the strength of your handshake, which also has a distinct impetus to the left. I infer that the typewriter you use has an unusually heavy carriage return, suggesting that it is an old model.'

'Well!' Jabez Hope exclaimed, 'I wonder if you can solve this mystery as quickly as you have determined my occupation.'

'We shall see,' remarked Holmes. 'Would you care to tell us something about it? Your letter was rather vague, though beautifully typed.'

'Of course,' said Jabez Hope. 'It is this.' He pointed at the station.

'I beg your pardon?' said Holmes, his brow furrowing.

'The station.'

'I need a little more to work with,' said Holmes, folding his arms.

'I am a railway enthusiast,' said Mr Hope, 'and I was delighted when I heard that there would be a line going out to Hampstead and beyond, as I live a few minutes' walk away. I envisaged Saturday afternoons on the platform with my notebook and a Thermos flask, noting the numbers of the trains as they arrive and depart, recording the livery, perhaps travelling to an interchange . . . '

'Your narrative rambles almost as far as some of these underground routes,' Holmes snapped. 'Would you mind arriving at your destination?'

'I do apologise.' Jabez Hope wiped his spectacles and replaced them on his nose. 'The romance of the railway carries me away, rather. As I said, I had high hopes for the new station — but now it is here, and utterly deserted! It doesn't even open at weekends, and its service is extremely limited during the week, when half the trains do not stop here. In short, I do not see the point of it. But that is not all. I believe that there is' — he looked around the empty street, then lowered his voice — '*something going on.*'

Holmes looked round too, and leaning towards Mr Hope, whispered, 'I believe that you are making a mountain out of mere bureaucratic incompetence!'

'Oh really?' Jabez Hope raised his eyebrows. 'Then I'll tell you something that may make you think again. I have never got as far as the station platform. The stationmaster will not sell me a ticket; he always tells me that there are no trains stopping for over an hour, or till the following day. Once I waited for an hour, just to see what he would do. Five minutes before the train was due he called me over, told me that all trains were cancelled because of an incident, marched me out, and closed up!'

'That does sound rather odd,' Holmes mused. 'Let us go in.'

The station seemed normal enough; still shiny and new, and rather fine with its pale blue tiles. Holmes took a step towards the staircase and —

'Hoi! Where do you think you're going?' An official in a peaked cap stepped into the ticket hall.

'Told you,' muttered Jabez Hope.

'Onto the train, naturally,' Holmes replied. 'May I purchase a ticket?'

The railway official gave Holmes a withering stare. 'No, you may not, sir. No trains to be had today, so I'm shutting up shop. Come back tomorrow.'

I consulted my timetable and stepped forward. 'But this clearly says — '

'Incident on the line at Hampstead, sir.' The stationmaster tutted. 'Terrible. Leaves from Hampstead Heath got down a ventilation duct, you see. Veeeeeery dangerous. Happens all the time.' And he shooed us out of the station.

'I begin to see your point, Mr Hope.' said Holmes. 'Would you pop back into the station and start an argument with that man, while I investigate further?'

Jabez Hope grinned. 'I shall enjoy that.'

He strolled back into the station. I heard a cry of 'Not you again!' before Holmes hurried me away.

'There is always another way,' he said, drawing out a set of lock-picks and setting to work on the stout oak door outside. Two minutes later it opened noiselessly onto a well-lit Axminster-carpeted staircase leading into the bowels of the earth. We descended, grateful for the thick carpet which muffled our feet.

'What do you think we'll find down here?' I whispered.

'I have no idea,' Holmes whispered back.

At the bottom was another oak door. Holmes put his ear to it, and his frown disappeared. He tried the door, then rapped hard, and shouted 'Come on, open up!'

'Holmes, what are you doing?' I cried.

'Family business,' Holmes smirked.

The door was opened six inches by a young man in office garb, holding a notebook. He opened his mouth but Holmes held up his hand. 'I'm here to see brother Mycroft.'

The man opened the door just wide enough to admit us into a cavernous room filled with desks, shelves, cabinets, and clerks. He led us down the central aisle to a large mahogany desk behind which sat Mycroft Holmes, dictating to an amanuensis. An expression of annoyance crossed Mycroft's face at the sight of us. He waved the secretary away and pointed to two chairs rather less luxurious than his own.

'Sherlock, I am rather busy, you know.'

'Bored with Whitehall, are we?' said Holmes.

'Not at all.' Mycroft Holmes shifted in his chair. 'I've just outgrown it.'

'In what way?' Holmes leaned forward.

'I am getting on in years,' said his older brother, reaching for his pipe. 'I will not be able to get the country out of its various messes for ever, and I suspect that there are plenty more messes to come. I put this to the Ministry, and together we came up with a plan.' He waved at the vast room. 'What you see here is the inside of my head. We are cataloguing the contents of my brain, establishing a network of knowledge which I hope will serve the nation for many years.'

'But why here, in an underground railway station?' I asked, incredulous.

Mycroft Holmes gave me the kind of indulgent smile you might bestow on a small child. 'Space, Watson. How much would this set-up cost on the surface of central London?'

'Ah.' I nodded. 'What about the noise from the trains, though?'

Mycroft pointed at the green baize lining the walls. 'Soundproof. Believe it or not, the platform is on the other side of that door.'

'So it is a working underground station?' Holmes asked.

'Of course! How else would I get here?'

'You lazy dog, Mycroft!' cried Holmes with a grin. 'This is on the same line as Leicester Square, five minutes from your house!'

Mycroft Holmes grinned back. 'Dear brother, you are

quite correct. I stroll to the station, board the "out-of-service" train, arrive here ten minutes later and set to work. So convenient . . . '

'And how long do you intend to commandeer this station?' Sherlock asked, wagging a finger. 'There are other people who would like to catch a train too, you know. You're only drawing attention to yourself.'

'That's a bit harsh, Sherlock,' Mycroft protested. 'I do let the occasional train stop, you know. Every other day or thereabouts.' He sighed. 'All right. Maybe one an hour. But I'll use this station as long as I need to for the good of the country, commuters or not!'

'Speaking of commuters,' said Holmes, 'the chap who put me on to this seems like a methodical sort of man. Very observant, and works in an office. Are you hiring at present?'

Mycroft looked shifty. 'I might be. Give me his name, and I'll think about it.'

We arrived back on the surface to find Jabez Hope holding a bloodied handkerchief to his nose. 'I shouldn't have made a run for it,' he said. 'The stationmaster rugby-tackled me on the stairs.' I instructed him to pinch the bridge of his nose. 'Did you find anything?' he asked, nasally.

'We did,' said Holmes. 'I cannot divulge more at present, except that there is no need to be concerned. I suspect you may hear more presently, but for now, Mr Hope, you must pursue your train-related activities

80

elsewhere.'

Jabez Hope's smile was just detectable under his handkerchief. 'That's quite all right, Mr Holmes. After all Camden Town, which is an *interchange*, is only seven minutes' walk away.'

Two months later, over dinner, Holmes read me a letter from Mr Hope thanking us for our help. The address was given as 'Adjacent to Platform 2, Mornington Crescent.' Apparently Mr Hope is enjoying his new work immensely, the stationmaster is quite a nice man when you get to know him, and Mycroft Holmes's typewriters are brand new Underwoods. I would have expected nothing less.

The Case of the Secret Code

As I opened the front door of 221B Baker Street I couldn't help feeling that all was right with the world. I had dined well at my club, won a game of billiards against an extremely stiff opponent, and celebrated with some excellent port. I entered the sitting room and narrowly missed having my head taken off with the poker.

'Oh! It's you,' Sherlock Holmes exclaimed, stepping out from behind the door.

'What on earth are you playing at, Holmes?' I asked, somewhat testily.

Holmes leaned towards me and hissed. 'There's a plot, a plot to kill us both!'

I fell into the armchair, wishing I had held back a little on the port. 'Holmes, are you sure?' Without speaking out of turn, Holmes saw murder round every corner. Last month he had been convinced that our page Billy was in the pay of foreign spies, and marched him to the police station to be interrogated.

'Of course I'm sure — look!' Holmes brandished a sheet of pale blue paper. 'I found this on the pavement! All I need to do is crack the code.'

'Let me see.' I examined the paper, which appeared to be a hastily-scrawled list. It had suffered during the time it had spent outside; but the words 'Mr H' and 'Dr W' were legible. My head spun.

Holmes grabbed the sheet back. 'It seems to be an alphanumeric cypher.' He read, tracing the blurred characters with his forefinger. 'Under my name: Sh — 5, T — 2, UG — 2, Sks — 2. L — all, Sh S&I. What can it mean?'

'What does it say under my name?' I asked.

'The lower part of the writing has run, but I can definitely see Sh — 7, T — 4, UG — 7 . . . what is UG? Underground? And why would yours be 7 and mine 2? Ah, your bedroom is at the back of the house . . . perhaps they are planning to tunnel beneath Baker Street and murder us in our beds!'

'The bedrooms are upstairs,' I pointed out.

'True,' Holmes conceded. 'Could these be abbreviations for chemical elements? S and I would be sulphur and iodine — but those are harmless, and the other letters do not correspond. Yes, it must be a code.' He sat down at the desk, drew a notepad towards him, and lit his pipe. The next half-hour was silent except for the scratching of Holmes's pen and an occasional muttered curse.

The peace was broken by the slam of the front door, followed by Mrs Hudson's dulcet tones. 'This is most careless, Billy!'

'Billy has divulged information to our foe!' breathed Holmes.

Mrs Hudson hurried in. 'I apologise for disturbing you, gentlemen, but — oh!' I followed her gaze to the blue paper. 'In fact, everything is well.' She walked over and twitched the sheet out of Holmes's hand.

'Do you know something about this, Mrs Hudson?' thundered Holmes.

'Of course; I wrote it. It's a memorandum of your week's laundry. Shirts 5, trousers 2 . . . and so on.'

'What is S and I, Mrs Hudson?' I asked.

'Starched and ironed,' she replied crisply.

'And UG?'

'Undergarments,' piped Billy, who had followed Mrs Hudson into the room.

'Well, that's a relief,' I said, when they had departed. 'Although you might want to consider changing yours a little more often, old man.'

Holmes smoked his pipe in injured silence.

The Case of the Auburn Hair

'So, Watson, my monograph on cigar-ash is likely to become a key reference text — '

A tap at the door interrupted Holmes, and after some whispering outside, Billy appeared. 'Er . . . a lady to see you.' A heavily-veiled woman stepped forward.

'You may go, Billy,' said Holmes. 'Do take a seat, Mrs . . . '

'I would rather not give my name,' said the veiled figure, somewhat indistinctly.

'That will make it difficult for us to help you,' said Holmes. 'Could you at least lift your veil?'

The lady did so, revealing herself to be an attractive and extremely embarrassed young woman.

'I take it that you have not come to us about a criminal matter,' remarked Holmes.

The lady grew even redder. 'Oh, is it so obvious?' she cried. She hung her head and began to weep.

'I'm afraid your manner does rather give it away,' Holmes said in his most soothing voice.

'Give what away?' I asked, utterly bewildered.

'Oh, Watson,' said Holmes, as if to a naughty child, 'our guest suspects her husband of an affair.' He patted the lady on the shoulder. 'Shall I ring for some tea?'

The lady sniffled, and composed herself with an effort. 'No, no, thank you. As you have guessed so much already,' — Holmes bristled at these words — 'I shall tell you the whole story. My name is Mary Danvers. I was married almost a year ago and moved to Borehamwood with my husband. Until recently our life was idyllic, but over the last month there have been signs . . . that all was not well.'

'What do you mean, Mrs Danvers?' I asked.

'Well, first a letter came for my husband addressed in a strange hand; a lady's hand. I asked who it was from, and he brushed it aside. I searched for the letter when he went to work, but I could not find it. A week later he said that he had to take an overnight business trip, which is most unusual. When he returned I enquired about the trip and again he gave vague answers.' She broke off and regarded me with sad eyes. 'I see that you do not think much of my plight, Dr Watson.'

'No, no, not at all!' I protested. 'I — well — I just wondered whether there might be another explanation.'

'I have not finished,' said Mrs Danvers. 'When I unpacked his clothes, I brushed his jacket and found —

these!' She pulled a handkerchief from her bag and opened it to reveal two bright auburn hairs, no more than an inch long.

'Ah,' said Holmes.

'I couldn't bear to confront him. I hoped it was a solitary lapse. But another letter arrived two days ago. My husband stuffed it into his pocket, and the next day he told me he had to take another trip, the day before our wedding anniversary. I cannot stand any more of it. My heart will break!'

Holmes passed his handkerchief to Mrs Danvers and she sobbed into it. 'What would you like me to do?' he asked gently.

Mrs Danvers's eyes shone with damp fury. 'I want you to find this woman, this home-wrecker, and make her stay away from my husband!'

Holmes breathed deeply. 'Mrs Danvers, did you happen to catch a glimpse of the post-town the letters came from?'

Her response was instant. 'Yes, it was Guildford. We know no-one there.'

'And . . . may I take one of the hairs?'

'Of course.' She selected one and handed it over.

'I will begin my enquiries immediately, Mrs Danvers. Let us hope for a speedy resolution.'

'Yes, Mr Holmes.' The lady rose and pulled down her veil. 'Good day to you.'

Holmes and I exchanged glances once Mrs Danvers

had departed. 'Are you going to round up all the red-headed women in Guildford?' I grinned.

'Heavens, no,' Holmes replied. 'We can narrow the field a little more. There cannot be many women living in the area with, well, almost cropped hair, and particularly not of the social standing which the softness of this hair implies. Such a woman would be eminently noticeable.'

'Unless she wore a wig!' I broke in, triumphantly.

'Yes, Watson, in which case we would not have this.' Holmes waved the hair at me. 'I will send Wiggins of the Irregulars down to make enquiries, as I am almost wholly engaged on the Potomac River business.' He reached for a sheet of paper and began scribbling. 'Ring for Billy, would you.'

The crop-haired redhead was the proverbial needle in a haystack; two days' enquiry by Wiggins led nowhere. A telegram came for Holmes, and he shook his head as he read it out: 'Husband on trip will confront on return heartbroken.'

'You tried your best, Holmes,' I said, but he shook off my sympathetic hand.

There were no further telegrams, and Holmes scanned the papers every morning for reports of marital unrest in Borehamwood or red-headed women in Guildford. 'Nothing,' he said. 'I am almost tempted to write and enquire.'

However, the next morning he was spared the

trouble. Among the post was a thick cream-coloured envelope addressed to Holmes, postmarked Borehamwood. Holmes ripped it open, withdrew a deckle-edged card, and began to laugh uproariously.

'I do wish you'd tell me what's so funny,' I grumbled.

'The mystery redhead is revealed!' Holmes, still laughing, passed the card to me. It was a photograph of Mary Danvers and, presumably, her husband. They were both seated, smiling broadly, and between them, looking straight at the camera, sat a puppy. The photograph was inscribed 'Mr and Mrs Danvers on their first wedding anniversary, with their Irish Setter, Guildford Moonlight Sonata (Sherlock to the family).'

The Return of Moriarty

It was a beautiful spring day, and I felt uncommonly happy as I strolled through the park towards the residence of my old friend Sherlock Holmes. My wife was away visiting a schoolfriend, and Holmes and I had agreed that dinner and a concert would be a most acceptable way to pass the time. Mrs Hudson welcomed me, and we chatted in the hall before she opened the drawing-room door and announced, 'Dr Watson's — Oh!'

Holmes was huddled in an armchair, his knees drawn up to his chin, rocking slowly and staring straight ahead.

'Holmes, my dear fellow!' I advanced and touched him on the arm, but he shook me off.

I removed my hat and sat down. 'Leave me with him, Mrs Hudson. Perhaps time will bring him round.'

Mrs Hudson withdrew, and I poured myself a small whisky. Holmes's eyes followed the motion of the decanter, and he whispered, 'Brandy, please,' through parched lips. I put the tumbler to his mouth, and his teeth chattered on the glass before he gulped the contents down.

'What on earth has happened, Holmes?' I asked.

Holmes's gaze slid towards me. 'He has returned!' he croaked.

'Who?'

'*Moriarty.*'

'That's impossible.' I passed a hand over my brow. 'You threw him over the Reichenbach Falls!'

'He is back, I tell you!' Holmes's voice rose querulously. 'He rang the bell half an hour ago! In the absence of Mrs Hudson and Billy I answered the door, and there he stood!'

'What did he say?'

'I slammed the door before he could speak. I am in fear of my life, man — I did not stop to enquire after his health!'

The door-bell pealed once, and Holmes moaned. I rushed to the hallway, nearly upsetting Mrs Hudson in my haste, flung the door open, and stepped back with an exclamation of horror.

It was he, Moriarty! He was just as Holmes had described him on the eve of their last, fateful encounter, a tall, pale man with deep-set eyes buried under a high forehead. He began to fumble in his pocket. I banged the door shut before he could shoot and ran back to the drawing room.

'Holmes, you were right! Moriarty has returned!' I poured myself a slightly stiffer whisky.

The letterbox rattled, and Mrs Hudson entered the drawing room, looking somewhat ruffled. 'The gentleman outside has just posted this, sir,' she said, handing Holmes a card.

Holmes read out loud, 'I have come to apologise,' and flipped the card over. 'Reverend Caleb Moriarty, MA.'

'Shall I show him in?' asked Mrs Hudson.

'Please do,' said Holmes. 'Watson, keep your revolver handy,' he muttered.

We agreed afterwards, over rather a good late supper, that our mistake had been quite natural given the cousins' strong resemblance. Reverend Moriarty was a most pleasant companion, and after a heartfelt apology for his cousin's deplorable conduct, he shared many amusing anecdotes of childhood holidays where his cousin's criminal tendencies were already becoming apparent. 'Watson, if you ever have children, let this be a lesson to you,' Holmes slurred. 'Villainy may begin with something as minor as an extra helping of pudding. Go on, Reverend, tell me the one about the frogs again.' And the Reverend, flushed and smiling, duly obliged.

The Case of the Vanishing Blueprint

When I recall the many cases I have delineated as Sherlock Holmes's biographer, some spring to the memory not because of the severity of the crime committed, nor the extent to which they demonstrate Holmes's deductive powers, but for another reason entirely. *The Case of the Vanishing Blueprint* is one such, and I document it without apology.

The events I will describe took place in 1882, during a dull, close August afternoon of the kind which signals an approaching thunderstorm. My old war wound was aching, Holmes was without a case, and in short, we needed a diversion. So when Billy appeared at the drawing-room door, we were delighted to see him.

'Mr, er . . . '

'Jones,' said a young, eager man, bounding forward

like a puppy. 'That's the name.'

'You may go, Billy,' said Holmes. 'What's your real name?' he asked, conversationally.

The young man deflated into a chair. 'I can't say . . . you never know who's listening! Anyway, my name is not important,' he declared. 'What matters is that a valuable piece of my property has been stolen!' He pronounced the last words triumphantly, and began to perk up.

'Why not go to the police?' I asked.

'The police? Are you mad? Everyone knows you can't trust the police!'

Holmes leaned against the mantlepiece. 'Do calm yourself, "Mr Jones". Can you tell me what has been taken?'

'Of course. You're right.' Mr Jones composed himself, with effort. 'It is the blueprint for my Patent Collapsible Hat! They've got hold of it somehow and all my hard work will be for nought!'

'Who has got hold of it?' Holmes inquired.

'Why, Them!'

'But if you have the patent, They cannot benefit,' I said, perhaps a little smugly.

The young man waved a hand. 'No, no, "Patent" is merely in the title of the Hat. I am still seeking a patent for my invention.'

'When did you last see your blueprint?' Holmes asked, assuming the 'consulting detective' manner I knew so well.

'Hmm . . . I definitely had it yesterday afternoon, at my desk, because I made a further modification to the springs. Then I went to the opera with my wife, and when I went to my desk this morning it was gone! Months of work!'

'Do you have any servants, Mr Jones?'

'No, no.'

'Had anyone forced their way in?'

'Absolutely not. Nothing was disturbed. Oh!' A sudden horror disfigured the young man's face. 'It was my wife, Maud! She has taken it!' He leapt out of his chair. 'Oh, the treachery!'

'Wait, wait!' I cried, putting a restraining hand on Mr Jones's arm. 'You are jumping to conclusions!'

'Dr Watson is right,' said Holmes, leading the young man back to his chair. 'Now, can you tell us about this Patent Collapsible Hat of yours? Is this one?' He gestured towards the rather squashed article on Mr Jones's head.

'It is!' cried Mr Jones, removing it. 'This is the prototype. Of course this is the hat in its collapsed state, suitable for everyday use. For formal occasions or evenings out, it transforms into a top hat with just a few simple adjustments. You pull this, and twist this, and — there!' The crown of the hat sprang upward, and a paper scroll fell out of the bottom.

'Well,' said Holmes, picking up the scroll. 'I think that

resolves the matter.' He unrolled the paper. 'Ah yes indeed, the Patent Collapsible Hat. And what is this other piece of paper?' He read aloud, 'Thoughts on a Method of Worldwide Networking and Information Sharing.'

'I'd prefer it if you didn't read any further,' said Mr Jones, snatching back the papers. 'I haven't worked out all the detail yet.'

'Perhaps you should stick with the hat,' laughed Holmes. 'Good day to you, sir.'

The Case of the
Red Neckerchief

My feet echoed on the cobbles, keeping time with the beat of my thoughts. *Don't let Holmes down, don't let Holmes down . . .*

Holmes's instructions that afternoon came back to me. 'Watson, I have rather a strange favour to ask, but your help in this case is vital.'

'You know you can ask me anything,' I said, pouring myself a whisky.

'Watson, I need you to threaten me in the street.'

My mouthful of whisky went straight across the room. 'What?!'

'Perhaps I should explain,' laughed Holmes. 'As you know, I have hardly been at Baker Street lately. A minor but interesting case has occupied me. I have infiltrated a protection racket which has half the shopkeepers in the Old Kent Road quaking with fear; in itself no small matter. I nearly have the ringleader, a creature called Fred Ketch, and if I have my way he will meet his brother Jack Ketch sooner rather than later.' I smiled at his sally. 'His crimes thus far are unknown, but the vile nature of the threats I have witnessed as his accomplice — well, I will not describe them to you.'

'I can imagine,' I shuddered.

'You can't.' Holmes consulted his watch, and rose. 'It is time for me to assume the character of a villainous hawker at a Southwark tavern where I keep a room. Watson, you will arrive at the Castle Inn at ten to nine this evening, wearing your shabbiest clothes. You will find me outside with Fred Ketch, as I have arranged a rendezvous to discuss expansion plans. You will know me by my red neckerchief.'

'Red neckerchief,' I repeated. 'Got it.'

'You will rush up and exclaim that despite all the money you've paid me, your workshop has been ransacked. Then you will grab my shirt and shout in my face. At this point I expect Fred Ketch to pull a knife, and the policemen concealed about the scene will arrest him. He always carries a notebook in which he records his business, and I suspect that its contents will be more than enough to put him behind bars.'

'You're sure this plan is safe, Holmes?' I asked. 'I wouldn't normally go south of the river at that time of night.'

'Of course!' cried Holmes. 'What could go wrong?'

My pulse was far quicker than usual when I marched down the Old Kent Road in search of my quarry. There he was! Holmes had become a workmanlike figure in a patched shirt and rough serge trousers. His red neckerchief flamed against his brown skin, and a covered basket lay at his feet. He conversed with a swollen, red-faced man who leered at passers-by with a laugh that gurgled like the Thames ooze.

I took a deep breath and strode over to Holmes. 'You!' I shouted, and took hold of him. 'Your protection is worthless! My workshop has been burgled and all my tools have gone!' I shook Holmes a little, to drive my point home. 'What do you have to say for yourself?'

'You what?' said Holmes. 'Don't know what yer talkin' about. Get off me!'

'I will not!' I shook him again and glanced towards Fred Ketch, who watched me beady-eyed. 'What are you going to do about it?'

Fred Ketch cleared his throat. 'You should get yer facts straight, mate. Let 'im go.'

'What? No!' I shook Holmes until his teeth rattled. 'I — want — my — money — back!' I let go and he sank to the cobbles, coughing.

'RIGHT!' Fred Ketch stepped forward. 'I'll deal with you meself!' He lunged at me and bent my arm up behind my back. 'You come along, now. We've got business in that alleyway . . . important business.' His grip was like iron as he frogmarched me down the alley beside the inn.

'Please don't hurt me!' I whimpered. Where were the policemen? I tried to twist round, but Ketch gave my arm an extra yank.

''URT you?' He flung me forward into the darkness and I fell on hands and knees. I braced myself for the slither of steel between my ribs.

Then I heard a snort. 'Watson, you idiot!'

I turned my head, and there was Sherlock Holmes, unstooped but still enormous and red-cheeked. He pointed to the scarf around his neck, which was so dirty that it appeared brown.

'Holmes! My God!' He helped me up. 'Then who was the man I — oh!' I staggered and would have fallen if Holmes had not caught me in his arms.

'Watson, you are one of the few men who has threatened Fred Ketch and got away with it. I had to stay in character but I feared for your life, even with policemen standing by.' Holmes gently stood me upright, and gave me a swig of brandy from his hip flask. 'Hop over that wall, and then you must get a cab home, and burn those clothes.'

I took a step or two. My legs seemed to hold up quite well. 'And what about you, Holmes?'

Holmes' eyes glittered. 'I shall head back down the alley and implement Plan B.' And with a wink he was gone.

The Case of the
Delicate Matter

I have wrestled with my conscience before in recording matters here which perhaps should remain confidential. This case, though, has caused me the most anguish of any. I have resolved to set out as much of the matter as I can, but in the interests of national security certain aspects must be redacted.

*

It was a rainy Sunday afternoon in November, and Holmes and I were engaged in indoor pursuits. Holmes was reading the *Police Gazette*, while I was updating my scrapbook of press cuttings. I had just pasted in an article from the *Herald* featuring rather a fine daguerreotype of Holmes, when Billy stumbled in, stammered, 'There's a gemmun to see you — a proper one!', and scarpered.

The gentleman advanced, and Holmes and I stood up at once. Who does not revere Lord _____, Minister of _____ and _____? Who has not read his speeches in the papers and cheered?

We shook hands, and the lord regarded his sticky palm with some distaste. 'I must apologise for disturbing your repose, but this matter is of the utmost urgency. It concerns the royal family, and in particular Princess _____.'

My mouth fell open. Princess _____, the nation's darling! 'What has happened?' I cried.

'Oh, she is safe,' Lord _____ replied. 'For now. As you know, the royal family are touring Ruritania. I received a telegram an hour ago which indicates that there has been a bit of a faux pas. The Ambassador took the family for a drive to view a flock of lesser-spotted _____, which are rare and revered in Ruritania. On viewing the _____, the princess remarked, "Oh, they are just like my mittens!" These were, indeed, made of lesser-spotted _____ fur. The mood in the carriage plummeted below freezing, and in short, we are afraid that there may be repercussions.'

Lord _____ and I both looked towards Holmes, who was nodding sagely. 'For heaven's sake, man, help us!' the lord pleaded. 'This problem needs the greatest mind we can bring to bear!'

Holmes leaned an elbow on the mantelpiece and filled his pipe. 'So what you are saying, Lord

102

_____, is that a young girl's innocent remark may cause an international incident.'

Lord _____ collapsed into a chair. 'That's exactly it.' He mopped his brow with a large monogrammed handkerchief.

Holmes lit the pipe and puffed at it for a few moments. 'As I see it, you have three options. Number one: admit the mittens were made from a lesser-spotted _____, say that no offence was meant, and hope it blows over.'

'Keep going,' said Lord _____.

'Number two: state that yes, Princess _____ did mean to insult both the lesser-spotted _____ and Ruritania, and prepare for war.'

The minister's jaw dropped. 'And number three?' he quavered.

Holmes smiled. 'Tell them that the mittens were made from artificial fur as a tribute to the noble lesser-spotted _____. Then burn the mittens before anyone can examine them!'

Lord _____ leapt up and pumped Holmes's hand. 'I knew you would arrive at a solution! The other ministers said you were a glorified bobby, but my faith in you is amply justified! I will put matters in train at once!' The door slammed behind him, and his horse galloped away.

'Ministers — pfff!' Holmes huffed. I think the bobby comment had rattled him somewhat.

Any future reader will know that Holmes's advice prevailed. War did not break out, and the royal family returned safely to Britain. Some months later a small package from Ruritania arrived at Baker Street. It was a medal for wildlife conservation and industrial enterprise, as displayed in the first Ruritanian lesser-spotted _____ artificial fur factory. Holmes awarded the medal to the skull on the mantelpiece.

The Case of the Giant Rat of Sumatra

'Holmes, will you play me another of those *Lieder* before we retire?' I asked, closing the curtains.

Holmes tucked the violin under his chin and reached for the bow, but a ring at the door forestalled him. 'Now, who would call at this hour?'

We waited. 'Perhaps Billy has gone to bed,' I remarked.

'Mrs Hudson will answer, then.'

Presently we heard the stairs creak. The door opened, and we heard the murmur of low voices. 'Well, come on!' Holmes muttered, watching the sitting-room door.

Mrs Hudson knocked and entered, her cap askew. She was followed by a man so muffled in hat and scarf that only his eyes were visible. 'A gentleman to see you, Mr Holmes. He won't give his name but he assures me it's urgent.' She sighed. 'Will that be all for tonight?'

'Yes, Mrs Hudson, thank you.'

'Good.' The door banged behind her.

'I do apologise,' our visitor said, pulling his scarf down slightly. 'Both for the mystery and for the lateness of my call.'

'That's quite all right, Sir Joseph. Do take a seat.' Holmes indicated the sofa.

The man jumped. 'How do you know my name?'

'It is my business to know things,' Holmes smirked. 'I rather wondered when you would visit. Your excessive concealment confirmed my supposition that you would not entrust such an important matter to a subordinate.'

I rubbed my forehead. 'Holmes, would you mind explaining?'

'Of course. I take it you do not read the *Daily London Messenger*, Watson?'

'That rag?' I spluttered. 'Never! I wouldn't clean my shoes with it!'

'Perhaps not,' Holmes remarked. 'However, many people read and, in some cases, even believe its sensational stories. It has the largest circulation of any London newspaper. The latest bee in its bonnet is this.' He opened the *Times* lying on the table, drew out the *Messenger* hidden inside, and tapped the front page.

'GIANT RAT OF SUMATRA FOUND IN LONDON SEWERS,' I read. 'Omnivorous Monster Threat To Women and Children.' Below the headline was an engraving of a huge rat, teeth bared, leaping at a screaming woman. The rat and the woman were almost the same size. 'Good heavens!' I cried.

'Now, Watson, you will understand why Sir Joseph Bazalgette, the chief engineer of the Board of Works, has come to see us.'

'They've started a petition to close my sewers,' Sir Joseph grumbled. 'The paper says that the sewers are causing the rat problem. I've been to their offices, and they won't tell me who supplies their information. All the paper says is "a concerned informant". I'm concerned for the health of London! Cholera might return if the sewers close!'

'And the Great Stink,' I interjected. 'Nobody wants that to happen.'

'Quite,' said Holmes. He rose and replaced his violin in its case. 'Well, there's no time like the present. I propose we visit the sewers and form our own opinion.'

'Holmes, is that strictly necessary?'

'When the *Daily London Messenger* reports something, Watson, that does not make it false. I prefer to see with my own eyes.' Holmes opened the door, and we ventured into the night.

Sir Joseph led us to the Edgware Road, opened the sewer cover with his stick, and we descended into the bowels of London. 'Ugh!' I cried, as the smell assaulted my nostrils. I had donned stout boots, but the foul water was rising over their tops.

'Ssh!' Holmes hissed. 'Look — a light!' He pointed to a faint glimmer in the circular brick tunnel. 'Someone is down here!' We sloshed along as quietly as we could, Holmes leading the way.

Then we gasped. Outlined on the wall was the shadow of a giant rat, fully five feet tall.

'Good God!' I choked. 'It is worse than we feared!' I clutched at Sir Joseph's arm for support.

'Someone may be injured!' cried Holmes. 'We must help them.' He approached the shadow, and we saw the enormous nose twitching. 'Ha!' He dived to the floor and we heard thrashing water. I ran forward, stick raised, to protect my friend, and Sir Joseph ran with me.

Holmes got to his feet. 'Allow me to present *Sundamys infraluteus*, the Giant Rat of Sumatra!' He held up a speckled brown rat, perhaps a foot long.

'It's hardly giant,' I said. The rat stared me down.

'Everything's relative,' Holmes chortled.

'Oi!' A voice echoed round the sewer. 'I was drawing that!' A small man in a flat cap and fishing waders appeared, carrying a lantern and a sketchbook. 'I had 'im down lovely,' he remarked wistfully.

'Ramsbottom of the *Messenger*, I believe.' Holmes stretched out his free hand for the sketchbook, and displayed a pen and ink drawing of a giant rat with a child in its jaws. 'Not a bad likeness,' he said, comparing the whiskered sitter with its portrait.

The little man drew himself up. 'The circulation's gone up by half since we began the rat campaign, thanks to my reportage sketches.'

'Well, this is where it stops,' said Holmes. 'The three of us are witnesses, and we have the rat. Cease your scaremongering —'

'Yes, and drop your petition!' Sir Joseph cried. 'You're a threat to public health!'

'All right,' Ramsbottom sighed. Then his face brightened. 'I could do a lovely headline for tomorrow.' He made quotation marks with his fingers. '"SHERLOCK HOLMES VANQUISHES GIANT FLESH-EATING RAT IN SEWER BATTLE." I can do you strangling the rat with your bare hands, if you give me ten minutes . . . '

'No, thank you,' Holmes said, gripping the rat firmly.

'It would go on the front page, you know.'

'NO!' Holmes's voice rang round the tunnel. 'I bid you good evening.' He stalked away, sloshing as he went.

'Holmes!' I called. 'What about the rat?'

Holmes looked down at the rat, who looked up at him and began to wash its face. 'I shall name him Ramsbottom. Don't tell Mrs Hudson, there's a good fellow.'

The Case of the Whispering Policemen

'Watson, we must go to Scotland Yard,' Holmes announced, leaping up and flinging on his coat.

'Bwah!' I cried. Holmes had been lying motionless on the sofa for half an hour, and I had assumed he was asleep. 'I didn't know you had a case at present.'

'I haven't,' he said. 'Not since I solved the small matter of the beryl coronet the other day. However, I have a distinct feeling I am needed there. I may not be wanted there; but that's entirely different.'

He took the stairs two at a time, and I hurried after. 'Holmes, you never go to the Yard except by invitation. What's going on?'

Holmes whistled for a cab. 'When I visited the other day, I detected . . . ' he lowered his voice, '*undercurrents*.' A hansom cab stopped and he jumped in.

'What sort of undercurrents?' I asked, taking my seat beside him.

'Whispering in corners, that sort of thing.' Holmes looked out of the window.

'But who? Policemen?'

'Yes! I am concerned for Lestrade. I heard his name several times, but whenever I identified the speaker he scurried off. And I am convinced at least two of them mentioned the tenth, at two o'clock.'

'Why, today is the tenth!' I looked at my watch. 'And it's a quarter to two now.'

'Congratulations, Watson,' said Holmes. 'We are almost at the Yard.' He rapped the ceiling with his cane. 'I think it best to be on the spot, in case Lestrade needs help.'

We alighted at the Yard and walked through the imposing green doors. I am no detective, but even I could see that something was not as usual. Instead of bustling about, officers were talking in small groups. Occasionally one checked his watch. At ten to two a group hurried away.

'It does look fishy, Holmes,' I muttered. 'You were right to come.' Holmes's jaw was clenched, and I feared for any policeman who would dare to transgress while he was on the premises.

'Excuse me, Mr Holmes, do you have an appointment?' The imposing figure of Sergeant Ribstock approached us.

Holmes walked up to the sergeant and stood tall. 'I am generally welcome here.'

Sergeant Ribstock didn't move an inch. 'Of course, Mr Holmes, but we are rather busy this afternoon. If you will take a seat,' — he waved a hand at some chairs in the corner — 'I will see if you can be attended to.'

'If you are all so busy — not that you seem it — I will take my leave. Good day to you.' Holmes swept out, and I trailed in his wake. 'Quick!' He dashed round the side of the building and in at the yard entrance. 'Whatever it is, it will happen soon!'

We re-entered the main building and hid in a conveniently curtained alcove. A group of policemen marched past, looking from side to side. Several appeared to be concealing something beneath their tunics.

'I don't like this, Holmes,' My voice trembled. 'I don't like it at all.'

'Come on.' We tiptoed down the corridor after the men, who went into the third room on the left. The sign on the door said, 'Interrogation Room. Only to be entered by authorised personnel.'

Holmes consulted his pocket watch. 'One minute to two. I will scotch their scheming!' He flung the door wide and stepped inside. 'Why, it's completely dark!'

A match flared, and there was a groan of disappointment. 'It's 'im!'

'I knew he'd be on to us!'

We raised our canes and immediately were grabbed by what felt like a hundred hands. A rough palm clamped my mouth shut. 'Quiet now . . . '

The door opened again, and a familiar voice said, 'Well, what on earth can be going on here?'

A voice whispered 'One, two, three,' and the room yelled 'SURPRISE!' The lights went up and revealed a banner: 'Happy birthday, Inspector Lestrade!' Sergeant Ribstock came forward bearing a huge cake.

'Oh my!' grinned the Inspector. 'You've done it again, chaps!'

'Glass of rum punch, sir?' The sergeant indicated a bowl and mugs in the corner.

'Don't mind if I do!' A constable served him, while another started up a gramophone. A third presented a package tied with an elaborate bow.

Sergeant Ribstock ambled across. 'We surprise him for his birthday every year,' he said. His face was already flushed from the rum punch. 'He never suspects! One time we lured him to an empty house and hid in the attic. Good times, good times . . . ' He wandered back to the punch bowl.

'Nice of you to stop by, Mr Holmes.' Inspector Lestrade beamed at us. 'Although I don't believe Sergeant Ribstock invited you.'

Holmes coughed. 'Well, I had picked up on certain — signals — that something was afoot, so it seemed like the right thing to do.'

Lestrade motioned us closer. 'They do it every year, you know, the surprise thing. They love it.' He chuckled. 'Bless 'em, they never suspect I know what they're up to!'

Holmes stared at him. 'But why do you let them take you in, Lestrade?'

Lestrade tapped his nose. 'Mr Holmes, I'll let you into a secret of my own.' He lowered his voice until he was barely audible. 'Part of being a good policeman, and a good colleague, is humouring the people you work with.' He tipped me an enormous wink from the eye Holmes couldn't see.

'Quite so,' I replied, smiling. 'Quite so.'

The Case of the Diogenes Club

It was a balmy late-summer evening, when the heat of the day gives place to a refreshing breeze. I had had a busy day visiting various chronic cases, and returned to 221B to find Holmes sprawled on the sofa, newspaper in lap, staring into space.

'Busy day, Holmes?' I enquired.

'Thinking,' he replied.

'Jolly good,' I said. 'Shall I ring for tea?'

My hand reached for the bell-pull, but a gentle knock at the front door forestalled me.

Holmes snapped out of his reverie. 'That's Mycroft!' he cried.

'How do you know?'

'No-one else would knock as if the noise and action were so innately distasteful to them.'

'But he has never come here before,' I said. 'You always visit him.'

'Exactly!' crowed Holmes. 'This must be a most important matter!'

Thirty seconds later Holmes' hypothesis was proved correct. 'Mr Mycroft Holmes,' squeaked Billy, retiring hastily.

'Mycroft!' Holmes leapt up and pumped his brother's hand.

The weariness on Mycroft Holmes's face turned to disgust at the energy Holmes was expending. 'Do you have to be so effusive, Sherlock?'

'Take a seat, Mycroft. What brings you here?' Holmes flapped an impatient hand at me. 'Watson, the tea!'

Mycroft Holmes lowered himself into a high-backed chair. 'As you know, Sherlock, I rarely venture beyond the sacred triangle of my rooms, Whitehall, and the Diogenes Club. On this occasion, however, I have no choice.'

'Government business?' asked Holmes, casually.

'No, no,' said Mycroft. 'Much more important than that. There is a recurring — unpleasantness — at the Diogenes Club. As you will recall, silence is the rule there.'

I nodded. I had visited the club once and was now on my final warning, having broken the rules first by asking if I might borrow a match, and then by suffering an unmuffled coughing-fit.

'So, what has been going on at the Club?' asked Holmes.

'Noise!' declared Mycroft. 'Noise of a particularly distracting, invasive, and random kind. It has been going on for the last four days, but now things have come to a head. I went to the Club as usual this evening, and at first all was quiet. I selected a periodical, the latest edition of *Blackwood's*, and settled down to read. The noise began moments later. I buried my head in the magazine to try and shut it out, but it continued for quite five minutes. Eventually it ceased, but shortly afterwards a floorboard creaked nearby. I looked up to see my fellow club members gathered round my chair, pointing at me. No words were exchanged, but I knew that they were charging me, as co-founder of the club, with finding and eliminating the noise.'

'But Mycroft, your brainpower is second to none. Why have you come to me?' Holmes sounded genuinely mystified.

'Sherlock, I am an impractical, sedentary sort of fellow. I cannot be expected to creep along passages and climb into lofts. That is most definitely your sort of thing!' Mycroft sat back with a satisfied smile.

'What sort of noise is it, and where does it come from?' Holmes asked.

'Well, it varies. Sometimes from the floor, sometimes the walls, sometimes even above my head. A scraping, rattling, pattering noise . . . '

'Bats.'

'I am not!' Mycroft retorted.

'Bats, mice, or squirrels,' Holmes sighed. 'It isn't a detective you need, it's an exterminator.'

'Oh,' said Mycroft. 'How would I find one of those?'

'For goodness' sake!' Holmes strode to the writing desk, dashed off a note, and rang the bell. 'Billy, please send a telegram to Mr Jamieson, 51 Oliphant Street.' Billy nodded, and withdrew. 'Mr Jamieson is an expert, and indebted to me for a service regarding a missing diamond necklace, which Watson has documented in the *Strand* with his customary dramatic flair. He should call on you at the Diogenes Club at six tomorrow. Now, Mycroft, as I have solved your difficulty in a manner requiring you to make no effort whatsoever, it is your brotherly duty to treat us to dinner. I hear that Simpson's-in-the-Strand has some particularly fine beef in stock.'

'Well, Sherlock,' said Mycroft, rising with some difficulty, 'though your alacrity is enough to give anyone indigestion, I suspect that on this occasion you may be right. Call a cab, would you? I am quite worn out.'

The Case of the
Lost Stradivarius

'How is the Stradivarius case progressing, Holmes?'

'Oh, no leads. No leads at all. Still working on it, though.' Holmes fidgeted with a button on his waistcoat. 'It's a glorious afternoon, Watson, why don't you take a stroll in the park?'

'I might just do that,' I said. 'Will you join me?'

'I'm too busy thinking,' said Holmes. 'I'll see you at dinner.'

I mused on the case as I sauntered down the Broad Walk of Regent's Park. Mr Brown, one of the principal violinists of the Hallé Orchestra, had called at our rooms a week ago in great distress. His prized Stradivarius had disappeared during a train journey from London to Manchester. 'No other violin will do!' he said, woebegone. Holmes cross-examined the musician, and assured him that he would do his best to find the missing instrument. So far, though, he seemed to be drawing a complete blank. Even stranger, he didn't seem to mind.

My stomach informed me that it was almost time for afternoon tea, and I retraced my steps to the townhouses of Baker Street. The mild weather had permeated here too, and I heard the strains of a violin sonata floating towards me. Holmes must be taking a break from thinking. And yet there was something different about his playing. Something about the tone of the instrument —

I gasped, tiptoed upstairs, and crept up behind Holmes, who was lost in the beautiful sounds. I tapped him on the shoulder. Holmes jumped, laid the violin down reverently in its case, and closed it with a snap.

'Holmes, I believe you have some explaining to do.'

He opened and closed his mouth once or twice, then shrugged and sat down. 'It was ridiculously simple. Mr Brown told us that when he came to leave the train, his violin was not in the luggage rack where he had left it. We know that the stationmaster did not see anyone carrying a violin case, and Mr Brown informed us that the violin was not at the Manchester lost property office. The obvious conclusion was that someone had moved the violin to fit their own luggage in, and the violin had travelled on without Mr Brown. A visit to the lost-property department at St Pancras confirmed that the violin had made a return journey to London, and, well, here we are.' He reopened the case and ran his fingers over the honey-toned wood.

'You will give it back to Mr Brown, of course.'

Holmes sighed. 'Do I have to?'

'Holmes, you saw how upset the man was,' I remonstrated.

'I would never have left you in the luggage rack,' Holmes told the violin.

'Holmes . . . '

'All right! I'll send a telegram tomorrow. Just let me have another night with her.' Holmes cradled the violin under his chin and improvised a cadenza. 'What would you like to hear?'

'You know I love Mendelssohn.' I lay back in my armchair, closed my eyes, and listened with a clear conscience until Mrs Hudson arrived with our tea and fish-paste sandwiches.

The Case of the Social Network

'Holmes, have some supper.' I gave the bell a hearty tug. 'Starving yourself won't solve the case.'

Sherlock Holmes paused in his pacing for a moment, sighed, and shook his head. 'I can't see a way in,' he said. 'The leads don't lead anywhere!'

'Perhaps food will help,' I said. There was a light tap at the door. 'Here is Mrs Hudson now.'

'It's late for supper,' she reproached. 'I thought you'd forgotten.'

'I do apologise, Mrs Hudson,' I said, although it wasn't my fault and my stomach had been growling for over an hour. 'Mr Holmes is engrossed in a case.'

'Not again, Dr Watson!'

'I'm afraid so.' I drew myself up. 'A very challenging one. If you have any of Mr Holmes's particular favourites, do send them up. It may stimulate his brain.'

'I'll check the pantry.' Mrs Hudson scratched her ear. 'Would this case be anything to do with your visitor this morning?'

'Why yes, Mrs Hudson, it would.'

'Disappearing husband, is it?'

Holmes whipped round. 'Mrs Hudson, my clients' cases are confidential!' He stared at her. 'Are you acquainted with Lady Hargadon?'

Mrs Hudson grinned. 'I used to be.' She leaned against the doorframe. 'I knew her when she was Nelly Jebb, and not quite so fine as she is now. We lost touch after she went to be a showgirl, and now she won't give me the time of day.'

Holmes's mouth dropped open.

'She didn't mention that, then.' Mrs Hudson picked a thread from her apron.

'She most certainly did not!' Holmes rushed to the bureau and made a note.

'Mm. Well, for what it's worth, last Tuesday I had tea with a friend of mine, Millie Davis. We went to the new Lyons teashop in Piccadilly. Have you visited it, Mr Holmes?'

'I have not,' said Holmes, faintly.

'Oh, you should. Beautiful cakes they were, full of real cream. Anyway, Millie's housemaid is the cousin of Nelly Hargadon's scullery-maid, and Sir Maurice has been on several "business trips" lately, if you understand me.'

'I believe I do.' Holmes rushed to make another note. 'But how would the scullery-maid know that Sir Maurice wasn't really away on business?'

'She didn't, but Sir Maurice's secretary did. Sir Maurice asked him to book business trip tickets, and find someone to book the real tickets so they couldn't be traced back to him. Once Sir Maurice had waved the business tickets around, he got his secretary to cancel them. He's careful with money, you know.'

'But surely Sir Maurice's secretary wouldn't divulge the matter?'

'Of course not. But he got his friend Allen Jones to book the other tickets, which were for two people. And when his wife went through his pockets, to do the laundry, or so she said, she found them and he had to explain himself.'

Mrs Hudson took a breath. 'Now Allen Jones didn't give names, because he's a discreet chap. But Gertrude Jones knows who his best friend works for, and she put two and two together. I bumped into Gertrude in Marshall and Snelgrove's hat department on Saturday, and she told me the whole story. And here's the thing; she said the last set of tickets were one-way to Rome, with a suite at the Victoria for a week.'

Holmes stared at Mrs Hudson. 'How do you know Mrs Jones?'

'Oh, we were at school together.'

Holmes took a deep breath. 'Mrs Hudson, I don't suppose you know who Sir Maurice has run off with?'

'Well, I had words with the butcher yesterday, because the beef joint his boy delivered was maggoty. He did apologise, mind, and fetched me a new one, and just as I was leaving his daughter came in. I've known her since she was knee-high, spinning on one leg in the sawdust. She was pleased as punch because she'd just got into the front row of the chorus at the Theatre of Varieties. She's been in the back row for over a year, and she said she'd almost given up hope. But the night before, the middle front-row dancer didn't turn up, and Susan got her chance. And Susan said she wasn't surprised when this girl, Florrie Smith her name is, didn't show, because she had an admirer. Apparently she'd missed some nights already and the proprietor said she'd be out if it happened again, but Florrie said she didn't care and she was leaving the country soon anyway. And I must say that the replacement beef was much better. I can do you some cold with pickles if you like?'

'Thank you, Mrs Hudson,' said Holmes, looking up from his notes with a broad smile. 'That would be delightful.'

The Case of the Gory Corpse

Holmes and I were enjoying a post-supper pipe when several loud bangs sounded below. 'Someone is in urgent need of our services,' Holmes remarked, sitting up.

Billy appeared, and behind him was a panting, tweed-suited gentleman. 'Mr Sansom, sir,' gabbled Billy, before he was shoved out of the way.

'You have cycled here?' asked Holmes, glancing at the gentleman's knickerbockers.

'Yes, from Greenford, as fast as I could pedal.' Mr Sansom fell into a chair. 'Let me tell you what I have seen, and then you must accompany me there, and put a stop to the whole horrible business.'

Holmes poured a large brandy and passed it to Mr Sansom. 'In your own time.'

Mr Sansom took a draught of the brandy, and his breathing began to slow. 'I live in Harrow and often cycle around the countryside in the evenings, for pleasure and exercise. I was passing Greenford vicarage when I heard a bloodcurdling scream. I left my bicycle in the hedge and crept down the drive. Imagine my horror when through the window I saw the vicar standing over a young woman's body, grinning and holding up a bloody knife!'

'Good God, man!' I exclaimed, shocked out of my usual composure. 'Why didn't you go straight to the police?'

'I haven't finished!' cried Mr Sansom. 'I ducked down, to hide and recover myself, and when I looked again, a policeman was laughing with the vicar! He was in on it! The whole village may be part of this ghastly matter!' He shuddered. 'That's why I came straight to you. No matter how corrupt the local police force, I know Sherlock Holmes can bring the villains to book.'

'There is no time to lose,' said Holmes in his steeliest voice, retrieving his pistol from the drawer. 'We will take a cab to the crime scene and hope to catch them before they get away.'

We rattled through the streets, and the London bustle gave way to pleasant, if bumpy, country roads. Our hearts were too full of apprehension and loathing for speech. The cab lamps lit a signpost: 'Greenford, 1 mile.'

Holmes ordered the cab to wait around the corner, and we walked the last few yards to the vicarage.

Holmes yanked the bell.

The door was opened by the vicar himself, a mild-seeming man in shirtsleeves. 'What can I do for you?' he asked, yawning. 'I do apologise, I was just finishing my sermon for Sunday.' I recoiled, horrified at the show of goodness the fiend was putting on.

'Can you identify him?' Holmes asked Mr Sansom.

'Yes,' said Mr Sansom. His face wore an expression of utter bewilderment. 'He was the policeman!' He crumpled to the ground in a dead faint.

'What has been going on here?' asked Holmes.

The vicar blushed. 'I fear your friend has stumbled across a gruesome sight.'

'You monster!' I cried, and made to spring at him, but Holmes held me back.

'I am referring to the dress rehearsal of *Murder Most Gory*, the latest production of the Greenford Players.' The vicar ran a finger round the inside of his dog collar. 'We had booked the village hall but the heating failed, so I invited the company to rehearse here. When your friend comes round I can introduce him to our housemaid Tilly, who makes a very convincing corpse. Now, can I invite you gentlemen in for a nightcap?'

Mr Sansom stirred slightly, and moaned.

'Unfortunately, we have a cab waiting,' said Holmes.

'Perhaps you would care to attend the first night? I can send you tickets.'

'Excellent,' said Holmes, as we supported Mr Sansom

to stand upright. 'I think it will be very much to my taste.'

The Case of the
Olympic Athlete

It was early 1896 and Britain was Olympics-mad. The revival of the ancient Olympic Games had caught the public's imagination, and the newspapers had reported on the preparations until the athletes were as familiar as near relatives.

Even so, it was a distinct surprise when Billy rushed wide-eyed into the drawing room and announced, 'Horace Shackleton's here!'

'What? *The* Horace Shackleton?' I cried, jumping out of my chair.

'Who?' said Holmes, between puffs of his pipe.

'Oh, Holmes, don't you read the sports pages? Horace Shackleton, the Olympic coach!'

'Olympics? Have we gone back in time?' Holmes's disdain indicated that sporting events fell into the category of knowledge which he regarded as dispensable.

'Show him in, Billy,' I said.

Horace Shackleton entered, holding his cap in both hands. 'Mr Shackleton, what an honour. Do take a seat.' I indicated the armchair.

'I'd rather stand, if you don't mind,' he said, with a broad Yorkshire accent.

'How may we help you?' I enquired, as Holmes appeared more interested in his pipe than our visitor.

'I'll get to the point. Our Johnnie's been nobbled, and I need you gentlemen to get to the bottom of it!'

I gasped.

'And Johnnie is . . . ?' Holmes asked, raising an eyebrow.

'For heaven's sake, Holmes! Johnnie Matthews, our gold medal prospect in the hundred-yard dash!'

Holmes frowned. 'Why would you think that he's been nobbled?'

'The lad's going backwards! Right now I wouldn't put a shilling on him to reach the Olympic final next month!'

'You're a betting man, Mr Shackleton?' asked Holmes.

Horace Shackleton coughed. 'Well, sir, being as I started out in greyhounds, a bit of a flutter is almost expected.'

'And you apply the same principles to your athletes as

your greyhounds?'

'I do, sir. Balanced diet, plenty of exercise. Johnnie gets the same food as all the other athletes, but I think someone is doctoring it.' A shadow passed over his face.

'I take it Johnnie is well-known to the public?'

'Oh yes, the papers call him the housewives' favourite.'

'Indeed. I will come and see Johnnie in action tomorrow, if I may.'

We were at the London Athletic Club at eight the next morning, along with a crowd of spectators. 'Why are we here so early?' I grumbled. 'Mr Shackleton distinctly said nine o'clock.'

'Forgive me, Watson, I had a fancy to observe the crowd. Why don't you meet them at the changing facilities?'

I strolled down, and waited. Mr Shackleton arrived at eight-thirty, and we made awkward small-talk until the pavilion door opened at nine o'clock precisely. The famous figure of Johnnie Matthews entered and began stretching exercises.

Three minutes later, Holmes came in. 'I have solved your mystery, Mr Shackleton.'

'Already? Why, that's wonderful news! What have you discovered?'

Holmes drew himself up. 'You are both right and wrong, Mr Shackleton. Johnnie is indeed being nobbled!' He walked up behind the stretching athlete and lifted the tail of his shirt to reveal a flesh-coloured corset. 'He is growing fat through the kindness of his fan club! I have just seen him devour a slice of plum cake, a pork pie, and a chocolate eclair in five minutes flat! At this rate, you should enter him for an eating contest.'

Mr Shackleton rounded on Johnnie. 'Have you no self-control, lad?'

'It isn't my fault,' Johnnie whined, 'eating two boiled potatoes and a spoon of peas ain't natural! A man needs sustenance!'

'You can have that after the Olympics,' growled Mr Shackleton.

Holmes placed his fee on Johnnie Matthews at odds of ten-to-one, following a most unflattering photo of him in the *Telegraph*. Another photo, of a svelte Johnnie breasting the tape in Athens, now has pride of place on our mantelpiece.

The Case of the Christmas Cracker

'That's the best part of Christmas over,' said Holmes, leaning back in his chair. We regarded the half-eaten goose on the table.

'We did what we could,' I groaned. 'It was kind of Mrs Hudson to cook our Christmas meal before she left for her sister's.'

'It was,' Holmes sighed, 'but a goose for elevenses is quite hard to manage.'

We listened to the clock ticking on the mantelpiece.

'That's what I hate about Christmas,' Holmes grumbled. 'Such a waste of time. Nothing's open, and even the criminals are lounging around at home with their families instead of doing what comes naturally.'

'I doubt Lestrade feels the same way,' I laughed.

'Indeed,' said Holmes, in a way which suggested that

this was a failing on Lestrade's part.

'Come on, Holmes, let's go for a walk in the park,' I said, prising myself out of my chair. 'It might help us digest this bird.'

I opened the front door and met the eyes of a panting young man reaching for the bell. 'Gosh!' he exclaimed. 'You really are good, Mr Holmes!'

'I am Dr Watson,' I said, laughing.

'I take it this is not a social call,' said Holmes.

'No, it is not!' The young man's eyes almost popped out of his head. 'A calamity has happened, and I cannot understand how or why!'

'Do come upstairs,' smiled Holmes.

I settled the young man in the basket-chair and fetched a medicinal brandy. 'What has happened?'

'A ring has vanished — a valuable ring — an engagement ring! I was going to ask her today!' The young man clutched his head until his hair stood on end. 'It cost me all my savings!'

'Please try to stay calm,' said Holmes. 'Can you describe what has happened, Mr . . . ?'

'Smith. John Smith.' The young man gulped, and controlled his breathing with effort. 'I met the Honourable Amelia Berkeley last year at a ball, and our initial attraction has deepened into love. I have spoken to her father the Viscount, and after consideration, particularly of my financial circumstances, he has given the marriage his blessing.

'I planned to surprise Amelia with a proposal, and I hatched a clever plan. The family had invited me for a drink this morning, and in readiness I purchased a box of Christmas crackers from Harrod's. I operated on one cracker, the only golden one, to remove the novelty, then I inserted the ring and replaced the cracker in the box.

'I set off for Eaton Square with a light heart, and the Viscountess and Amelia received me in the drawing room. We conversed for perhaps half an hour, but I fear I was too excited to make much sense. I could only anticipate the wonderful surprise to come. The Viscount came in with Amelia's brother, who chuckled at my gift and proposed that we pull the crackers. I agreed, glad to speed the moment along, and Amelia went to fetch her sister.

'I brought the box of crackers in and offered them round, making sure I handed Amelia the gold cracker. The Viscount counted one-two-three and we all pulled the crackers together with a bang. The whole family squealed with delight as they scrabbled for their toys and put on their hats. I only had eyes for Amelia, who reached into the golden cracker, and pulled out — a silver thimble! The ring had vanished!

'I shook her cracker, but it wasn't there. I checked the carpet, and it wasn't there. I examined everyone else's novelties, but they were just the usual knick-knacks. The Viscount made a joke about Amelia remaining a spinster, but I was too wretched to laugh. I excused myself, saying that I had forgotten Amelia's present, and dashed to the nearest police station.

'I found the policemen playing blind-man's-buff. They said that I must fill in a form and they had run out. Then I noticed that the station was festooned with paper chains, and the policemen all wore paper hats. So I rushed to find you. Mr Holmes, I am a desperate man!' The young man regarded us mournfully.

'Most interesting,' said Holmes. 'There are a few points I would like to clarify, Mr Smith. You mentioned that you brought the crackers into the drawing room. Had you left the box somewhere, or had a servant taken it from you?'

'I left the box on the hall table. It was rather big and bright, and I did not want to carry it into the drawing room with me. How I wish now that I had!'

Holmes leaned forward and put a hand on the young man's arm. 'Never fear, Mr Smith, we will find your ring! I have just a few more questions. Did anyone else know your plan?'

'No,' John Smith sighed.

'You said that the Viscount had given the marriage his blessing. Were the rest of the family pleased at the idea?'

'I don't believe they knew, apart from the Viscountess, who has always been friendly towards me. Amelia's brother Jonathan is too busy learning the business of the estate to worry over his little sister, but we get along well enough. I don't suppose it matters what Hetty thinks.'

'Is Hetty the youngest daughter?' Holmes asked.

'Yes, she's four or five,' John Smith said carelessly. 'Why do you ask?'

'I'm just trying to build up a picture of the family, Mr Smith. I wondered if it was significant that the ring was swapped for the spinster's thimble, which would suggest bad feeling. However, the family sounds disappointingly well-adjusted.' Holmes rubbed his chin. 'Could the ring have fallen out of the cracker, either at your home or along the way?'

John Smith shook his head. 'I checked the box before I left it in the hall. I was left alone while I removed my coat, and I took the opportunity to check the cracker once more.'

'It couldn't have been the gleam of a thimble?'

'No, I took the ring out to be absolutely sure. Then I replaced it, closed the box, and went to the drawing room.'

Holmes considered for a moment. 'One more question. When Amelia went to fetch Hetty, was she absent for long?'

John Smith considered. 'A few minutes. You don't think *she* did it?' His face drained of colour.

'No, I do not,' said Holmes. 'But I now have a pleasing theory which I should like to prove correct.'

'Aren't you going to ask me what the ring looks like, or about the servants, or whether anyone else called, or if there are any secret passages?' Mr Smith seemed rather dissatisfied with Holmes's methods.

'I doubt I need to know any of that,' said Holmes. 'If my hypothesis is false, I may pursue those lines of enquiry. For now, we will proceed to Eaton Square.'

The cab sped down the deserted streets, its wheels muffled by snow. John Smith grew more jittery as we neared our destination, starting at every check to the carriage's progress.

'Holmes, how on earth are you going to manage this?' I asked. 'You can't just call on a viscount on Christmas Day!'

'We'll use the tradesmen's entrance,' said Holmes, unperturbed.

A harried-looking scullery-maid opened the door. 'Yes?'

'We are here on a mission,' Holmes declared.

'Missionaries? This isn't a day for preaching, you know, we're too busy.'

'No, no . . . ' Holmes pointed at John Smith and whispered, 'a romantic mission.'

'Oo!' The maid stepped aside. 'You'd better come in then. The family are in the drawing room.' She nudged Mr Smith. 'Miss Amelia's playing the piano.'

'Oh!' John Smith's face took on a rapturous expression.

'There is just one thing I must see,' said Holmes. 'Would you mind if I step into the hall?'

'Not at all, sir.' The scullery-maid called the cook, who called a page, and Holmes and I followed him through the house. 'Just as I thought,' said Holmes, as we reached the hall. 'Back to the kitchen we go.'

John Smith sprang up as we re-entered the room. 'Have you got it?'

'No,' said Holmes, 'but I know who has. Now all we have to do is speak to them . . . '

'I'm bo-o-o-o-red!' said a little voice, which turned out to belong to a small girl with long blonde hair and very pink cheeks.

'Would you like a florentine, Miss Hetty?' asked the cook.

'Yes please,' said Hetty, holding out a sticky hand.

'Just one, now,' warned the cook. 'You've already had lots of treats.'

Holmes signalled to John Smith, and approached the munching child. 'Miss Hetty, can you show me what was in your Christmas cracker this morning?'

Hetty stared at the detective with round blue eyes, and held out a red spinning top.

'And now,' Holmes spoke very gently, 'can you show me the other thing you found in a cracker today?'

Hetty's eyes grew even rounder. She put her florentine on the table and pulled out a blue ribbon tied round her neck. And on the end of the ribbon was —

'The ring!' cried John Smith, and squashed Hetty in an enormous hug.

'It's too big for me,' said Hetty, sadly. 'So I put it on the ribbon till I'm older.'

I shook my head in wonder. 'Holmes, you have surpassed yourself.'

'It was elementary,' said Holmes. 'Once I had established that the ring had been taken at the house, it was a simple matter of who and why. The spinster's thimble almost misled me until I learnt that the family approved of Amelia's suitor. Likewise, the Viscount would not bless the marriage if he knew his daughter opposed it. So that left the servants, who are much too professional, sensible, and well-treated to risk prison.'

'I'm still not with you, Holmes,' I said.

Holmes held up a finger. 'We are almost there. The family would know what the ring meant, as would the servants, who all know the reason for Mr Smith's frequent calls. There is just one person who might not understand the ring's significance, and would see it as what it essentially is; a pretty thing. Mr Smith thought he was alone in the hall when he examined the golden cracker. He was not!'

The entire kitchen gasped.

'A certain small person was in the hall and saw — we do not know how much — but enough to know that the golden cracker had something especially nice inside. So when the coast was clear, the small person exchanged what was in the cracker for the thimble in her pocket.'

'But the hall was empty!' cried John Smith.

Holmes shook his head. 'It *appeared* empty. That is why I wanted to see it; to confirm that the hall table was, as I suspected, large and covered with a cloth to the floor.'

'Oh!' the kitchen exclaimed.

'That was why I asked how long the Honourable Amelia was absent when she went to find her sister. The question was not meant to ascertain whether she had substituted the thimble herself, but to see whether Hetty was where she should be. I imagine Amelia had to search hard to find the owner of a sparkly new ring.'

All eyes turned towards Hetty, who was eyeing the plate of florentines. John Smith walked over to her and knelt down. 'Hetty, it will take a long time for that ring to fit you. But I think that ring would fit your big sister Amelia, and if it does I'll buy you a little ring of your own. Shall we go and see?'

Hetty nodded, and pulled the ribbon over her head. John Smith untied the ring, took Hetty's hand, and set off for the drawing room.

We waited silently, hearts in mouths, except for Holmes who selected a florentine from the remaining few. The piano music halted. Just as he bit the florentine, laughter and exclamation burst from the drawing room.

'She must've said yes!' breathed the scullery-maid;

and there was a hushed celebration in the kitchen too. Then the drawing-room bell rang. The housemaid answered it, and we waited for news.

'They've said to lay an extra place for Christmas lunch,' she whispered, and we all cheered.

After a bracing walk back through Hyde Park, I poked the fire and changed into my slippers. 'I imagine you're pretty disappointed in yourself, Holmes.'

Holmes raised an eyebrow. 'Why would that be?'

I grinned. 'Despite your dislike for the festive season and for romance, you have played both Father Christmas and Cupid today.'

'Very funny.' Holmes flung himself onto the sofa.

'Speaking of Christmas, I haven't given you your present.' I pulled a package from my medical bag.

Holmes examined the parcel, held it to his ear, shook it, and then gave in and opened it. 'A deerstalker!' he exclaimed.

'I thought it would be warmer for rural cases than a top hat,' I explained.

Holmes donned the hat and studied himself in the mirror. 'It fits admirably,' he said. 'How thoughtful! I have something for you too, Watson.' He opened the drawer of the occasional table and handed me a flat oblong package.

'Holmes, this is most unlike you!' I tore at the wrapping and uncovered a handsome maroon journal and a fountain pen.

'I thought that my chronicler might need a new supply of tools,' Holmes smiled. 'And I also think that it is time for a glass of port and a goose sandwich.' He fetched the decanter and we clinked glasses.

'Merry Christmas, Watson.'

'Merry Christmas, Holmes.'

Afterword

I'm not sure when I first met Sherlock Holmes, but he was certainly around a lot in the 80s, when I was growing up. There was Jeremy Brett as Sherlock on TV, the short-lived *Young Sherlock* series, the film *Young Sherlock Holmes*, Russ Abbot's 'Barratt Holmes' character, and of course my local library had the books. To quote Mark Gatiss, co-creator of the BBC TV *Sherlock* series: 'Everything is canonical'[1]. So the Sherlock Holmes you've read about in this book has probably been influenced by all these versions, as well as Sir Arthur Conan Doyle's original stories.

This book came about by accident. Last year I had an idea for a more serious book with Holmes as a main character, but I didn't feel experienced enough to pull off a whole novel. These stories were an outlet for the

---

1 Gwilym Mumford, 'Sherlock returns to the BBC: "He's definitely devilish"', *The Guardian*, 17/12/2011.

research I'd started and the fragments of Victorian trivia floating around in my head; an affectionate tribute to the original. Having explored Sherlock's funny side, I returned to my serious idea for NaNoWriMo, and now I have an 82,000 word draft waiting its turn for revisions. Be very afraid . . .

The stories I've written are fiction with a tiny bit of fact mixed in. Here are a couple of examples. Oscar Wilde did go to Magdalen College, and he did have a check suit; but I doubt his aunt (if he had one) ever made off with his notebook (again, if he had one). Bram Stoker was business manager of the Lyceum Theatre, but the *Speckled Band* play, by Conan Doyle himself, appeared in 1910 (probably without dancing girls). I've created a Pinterest board showing some of the sources and inspirations for the book; search for 'The Secret Notebook of Sherlock Holmes' on Pinterest.

Finally, I hope you've enjoyed reading the book as much as I enjoyed writing it. If you would like to leave a short review on Amazon, Goodreads or elsewhere, I'd really appreciate it.

Acknowledgements

I would like to thank the following small army of people, who helped me greatly in getting this book written, revised, and polished.

For taking time out from their busy lives to read and comment on the *Secret Notebook*, and cheering me up when I feared I had written the worst book ever: Helen Borking, Brian S Creek, Laura Dunaway, Judith Leask, Monica Mastrantonio, Gaynor Seymour, Alaura Shouse, Lesley Smith.

John Croall provided eagle-eyed proofreading and fact-checking, and also calmed me down when I was despairing over single versus double quotes (I know, I'll be able to laugh about it one day). Any anachronisms which remain are my fault entirely.

Huge thanks go, of course, to the late Sir Arthur Conan Doyle, without whom there would be no Sherlock Holmes.

And the last and biggest thanks are to my husband Stephen Lenhardt, who not only read the book but put up with me while I was writing it, and encouraged and supported me throughout. He deserves a medal at the very least, but a dedication will have to do.

Cover credits

Main font (and chapter headings): Macondo Swash Caps by John Vargas Beltrán — SIL Open Font License — OFL

Foil texture on lettering: www.myfreetextures.com

Background photo: www.photos-public-domain.com

About the Author

Liz Hedgecock grew up in London, England, did an English degree, and then took forever to start writing. After several years working in the National Health Service, a corporate writing course rekindled the flame, and various short stories followed, some of which have even won prizes. *The Secret Notebook of Sherlock Holmes* is an attempt to put her master's degree in Victorian Literature to good use.

Liz now lives in Cheshire with her husband and two sons, and when she's not writing or child-wrangling you can usually find her reading, running, or cooing over stuff in museums and art galleries.

You can also find her here:
Website/blog: http://lizhedgecock.wordpress.com
Twitter: http://twitter.com/lizhedgecock